At ✳ Issue

Anti-Semitism

Mark McKain, *Book Editor*

Bruce Glassman, *Vice President*
Bonnie Szumski, *Publisher*
Helen Cothran, *Managing Editor*

GREENHAVEN PRESS
An imprint of Thomson Gale, a part of The Thomson Corporation

THOMSON
GALE

Detroit • New York • San Francisco • San Diego • New Haven, Conn.
Waterville, Maine • London • Munich

For more information, contact
Greenhaven Press
27500 Drake Rd.
Farmington Hills, MI 48331-3535
Or you can visit our Internet site at http://www.gale.com

Cover credits: © CORBIS RM, Metaphotos

LIBRARY OF CONGRESS CATALOGING-IN-PUBLICATION DATA

Anti-Semitism / Mark McKain, book editor.
    p. cm. — (At issue)
Includes bibliographical references and index.
ISBN 0-7377-2356-4 (lib. : alk. paper) — ISBN 0-7377-2357-2 (pbk. : alk. paper)
    1. Anti-Semitism. I. Title: Anti-Semitism. II. McKain, Mark. III. At issue (San Diego, Calif.)
DS145.A599 2005
305.892'4—dc22   2004060561

Printed in the United States of America

Contents

Introduction

Although anti-Semitism is on the rise in many parts of the world, in the United Sates it has been largely marginalized. Anti-Semitic acts and speech have become unacceptable to the vast majority of Americans. Alan Dershowitz, a prominent Jewish lawyer and author, noted that during Bill Clinton's presidency, Jews served as cabinet members, Supreme Court justices, ambassadors, and congressmen. Dershowitz remarked, "In today's America, a Jew can aspire to any office, any job, and any social status. . . . American Jews are part of the American mainstream."

Yet despite the virtual elimination of anti-Semitism from the American mainstream, hatred of Jews has continued to thrive on the Internet. According to a June 17, 2004, Associated Press article on anti-Semitism on the Internet, "Purveyors of hate have found a potent tool in the Internet." Thousands of Web sites promoting the hatred and prejudice of anti-Semitism are only a click away. "Electronic hate is the dark side of technology, and anti-Semites have particularly taken to the medium," commented Abraham H. Foxman, director of the Anti-Defamation League (ADL), an organization that monitors all forms of anti-Semitism. Indeed, it is believed that of some four thousand Web sites known to promote racist and anti-Semitic messages, twenty-five hundred are based in the United States.

Protected by First Amendment rights and a tradition of free speech, hate Web sites are flourishing in America. Because the Internet can mask the identity of its users, it is easy for disseminators of anti-Semitic literature to publish their propaganda anonymously and cheaply, and reach millions of readers. Christopher Wolf, chair of the Internet Task Force of the ADL, has remarked that the Internet "promotes anonymous collaboration, which allows hate mongers and terrorists to exchange ideas, information, and plots online, out of view." Some agree with Wolf and argue that anti-Semitic Web sites even inspire people to commit hate crimes in real life.

While American officials agree that anti-Semitic Web sites are an increasing problem, they differ on how to deal with them. Some people have compared anti-Semitic Web sites to another virulent and harmful Internet presence, child pornography. These commentators have asked that if child pornography sites are subject to censorship and criminal prosecution, why should anti-Semitic hate sites not have the same restrictions? On the other hand, because the First Amendment guarantees freedom of speech, the United States tends to oppose treaties and laws that criminalize racist and anti-Semitic speech. As U.S. assistant attorney general Dan Bryant has said, "We believe that government efforts to regulate bias-motivated speech on the Internet are fundamentally mistaken." Bryant says that the U.S. government believes in the freedom of everyone to express their own beliefs and that there is value in allowing those with seemingly wrong or even repugnant opinions to express their beliefs. Bryant therefore believes the best way to fight anti-Semitic speech is through educating young people and fostering understanding and tolerance. Indeed, it has been suggested that the best way to combat hate speech is to expose the fraudulence of anti-Semitic Web sites and enlighten people on how hate speech is harmful to others. Several representatives to an international conference on human rights organized by the Organization for Security and Cooperation in Europe (OSCE) have advocated the creation of a multilingual Web site that would expose Internet sites and organizations that publish anti-Semitic hate speech, so that interested people could educate themselves about and protect themselves from such groups.

One strategy to reduce online anti-Semitism is to encourage the companies that provide access to the Internet, called Internet service providers (ISPs), to enforce existing provisions in their contracts with Web site owners that prohibit racist and anti-Semitic speech. This could effectively block or significantly reduce hate content on the Internet. Another way to attack Internet hate sites is through the courts. Although the expression of hate on Web sites is not illegal in the United States, the courts have put limits on freedom of speech when it threatens others with harm. In this way, over forty states have enacted hate crime laws. In 1996 the Department of Justice prosecuted a case where Asian students at the University of California were sent racist and threatening e-mails. This case resulted in a one-year prison sentence for the culprit who sent the offending e-mails.

It may be impossible to completely shut down all anti-Semitic Web sites in the United States and elsewhere in the world. But as Foxman has remarked, "the combination of law enforcement action and education outreach is an effective one-two counter-punch" in reducing anti-Semitism on the Internet. As anti-Semitic Internet hate speech increases across the globe, it may be useful to adopt recommendations made at the OSCE conference to use the Internet as a positive force to promote enlightenment and tolerance as a means of combating anti-Semitism. After all, anti-Semitism has been largely marginalized in mainstream America due to a concerted effort to promote tolerance, understanding, and human dignity, so it may be a useful strategy for combating it online. The viewpoints presented in *At Issue: Anti-Semitism* examine these issues along with the impact of anti-Semitism in the United States and throughout the world.

1

Anti-Semitism Is a Serious Problem Worldwide

Stephen Roth Institute

The Stephen Roth Institute for the Study of Contemporary Anti-Semitism and Racism, which has one of the largest collections of anti-Semitic and Nazi literature in the world, monitors anti-Semitism and racism and publishes an annual report on anti-Semitism, Anti-Semitism Worldwide.

Anti-Semitic violence and attitudes are increasing worldwide. Jews are being victimized by a new kind of anti-Semitism, in which all Jews are linked with Israel and thus blamed for problems in the Middle East. News media across the globe compare Israel's treatment of the Palestinians to the Nazis' treatment of Jews. Anti-Semitism is also linked to anti-Americanism, and Jews are accused of manipulating U.S. foreign policy to wage war against Arabs and Muslims. Some have gone so far as to claim that Israel was behind the terrorist attacks of September 11, 2001. This demonization of Israel only furthers anti-Semitism and fuels increasing attacks on Jews worldwide.

The year 2002 and the beginning of 2003 witnessed an alarmingly significant increase in the number of violent antisemitic acts and in other forms of antisemitic activity. A total of 311 serious incidents were recorded worldwide in 2002, 56 major attacks (i.e., attacks using violent means) and 255 ma-

The Stephen Roth Institute for the Study of Contemporary Anti-Semitism and Racism, *Anti-Semitism Worldwide 2002/3*, www.tau.ac.il, 2003. Copyright © 2003 by The Stephen Roth Institute. Reproduced by permission.

jor violent incidents (attacks without the use of a weapon), whereas in 2001 there were 228 violent incidents, 50 major attacks and 178 violent incidents. The 2002 figure even slightly surpassed the year 1994 which marked a peak in antisemitic activity in the 1990s.

An analysis of the nature of these violent acts shows a troubling tendency: Prior to the outbreak of the second intifada [Palestinian uprising] in September 2000 physical violence had been directed mainly at cemeteries and in 2001 at synagogues. In 2002, however, this pattern changed dramatically: the number of physical assaults on Jewish individuals, or on people who resembled Jews, almost doubled, from 57 in 2001 to 112. Synagogues were still high on the list with 103 acts, including 40 arson attacks, compared to 92 incidents in 2001, as were cemeteries and memorial sites—73 incidents. . . .

> *Political, economic and social developments . . . have created a strong anti-Jewish atmosphere in which taboos are being broken.*

Most antisemitic violence in 2002 took place in western Europe, with 31 major attacks (out of the 56 recorded worldwide), and no fewer than 147 major violent incidents (out of 255 worldwide). Most of the major attacks in western Europe took place in Belgium and France (25 out of 31), while major violent incidents amounted to 96 cases in these two countries and the UK [United Kingdom]. In North America and the former Soviet Union the numbers were also higher than in previous years, while in other regions of the world—Latin America, Africa, Australia and eastern Europe—they were lower or remained on the same level. . . .

Many factors coalesced to create this serious situation, and may be discerned in the fourth wave of violence. The opposition to the war on Iraq, which unites a variety of political forces, includes many of the same elements that vehemently opposed globalization. Both the anti-war and the anti-globalization movements intensified anti-American sentiments and pinpointed the Jewish communities and Israel as the perpetrators of the September 11 [2001, terrorist] attacks, which were the pretext for the US decision to attack the Muslim world—first Afghanistan, then Iraq—and as being behind the giant commercial companies and banks that have globalized the world economy. Thus, a so-called axis of evil was created, made up of the US and Israel and encompassing world, and particularly American, Jewry—a villainous, modern, well financed and technologically sophisticated power that has willfully imposed itself upon other nations. The use of force, even in self-defense, has reinforced the comparison of this "axis" and its leaders with Nazi practices, which symbolize the definitive modern evil. Hence, the obligation of European countries to the memory of the Holocaust, which in recent years seems to have become increasingly more of a burden, might be weakened.

These political, economic and social developments, coupled with Arab/Muslim radicals, Arab oil money and their struggle against the West, have created a strong anti-Jewish atmosphere in which taboos are being broken: questioning the uniqueness of the Holocaust is no longer inviolable in Germany: authorities turn a blind eye to violence, as was the case in France prior to the 2002 elections; and academic institutes ban Israeli colleagues—a troubling demonstration of the politicization of some of the world's most acclaimed universities. Prospects for change seem dim at present because the balance of antisemitism has shifted to the democratic, enlightened West, where left/liberal circles have found common ground with positions in the Arab/Muslim world. Since the voices that speak out against antisemitism are becoming scarcer, and antisemitism often lurks behind anti-Zionism, the demonization of Israel and the Jews and their portrayal as an evil force responsible for all the world's evils may take even further hold. . . .

The New Antisemitism

The linkage between events in the Middle East and violence against Jews worldwide, which culminated in the year 2000 in the outbreak of the second intifada, provoked a dramatic increase in anti-Jewish violence, particularly in Europe. No less troubling was the realization that scapegoating of Jews and of Israel was no longer restricted to the radical fringe of the political spectrum in many western countries but had been embraced by the mainstream media. An important role in this development was played by the UN World Conference on Racism in Durban in August 2001. In numerous meetings and in the official decisions of NGOs [nongovernmental organizations] Israel was singled out for condemnation. The dissemination of antisemitic materials and efforts to distort the Holocaust were an integral part of the anti-Israel campaign carried out at this conference.

Demonization of Israel is also linked to the notion of Israel and the Jews conspiring against Arabs and Muslims, and as the main obstacle to peace in the world; this theory lay behind the accusation that the Jews were responsible for the terrorist attacks of 11 September.

> *Scapegoating of Jews and of Israel was no longer restricted to the radical fringe of the political spectrum in many western countries but had been embraced by the mainstream media.*

A motif that resurfaced with the outbreak of the second intifada and which intensified during the year 2002, becoming further entrenched in the mainstream discourse, was that of Israel as the present bearer of Nazi ideology. The outcome of this line of thought is that Israel is a Nazi state and as such must be destroyed.

At the end of 2001 and during 2002, in the wake of the September 11 attacks and the beginning of the American anti-terrorist campaign, another dangerous phase of "blaming the Jews" emerged: the linkage between anti-Americanism and antisemitism. This was based on the idea that the Jews and Israel actually controlled the US government and were driving America to conduct wars against the Arabs and Muslims, first in Afghanistan and then the war on Iraq. . . .

The Demonization of the Jews and Israel in Europe

In many countries, the motif of nazification of the Jews/Israel—accusing them of using Nazi methods against the Palestinians, including mass killings—in order to carry out "ethnic cleansing"—has penetrated influential mainstream media. Since it is commonly accepted that no Nazi state should exist, nazification of Israel and the Jews delegitimizes the right of Israel to exist. . . .

In Europe, which seeks to make a break with its Nazi past, blaming the Jews for the Arab-Israeli conflict can almost be seen as an act of absolution. Thus, it appears that guilt feelings over the Jewish fate during the Holocaust have been shifted to the Palestinians and the Arab nations which suffered as a result of the establishment of a Jewish state in the Middle East. The Portuguese novelist José Saramago, who won the Nobel Prize for literature in 1998, was part of an international delegation of writers who traveled to Ramallah to observe the Israeli siege of Yasir Arafat's compound. According to Saramago in the 21 April 2002 issue of *El Pais*, a Madrid-based newspaper read throughout the Spanish-speaking world, the situation in Ramallah was "a crime comparable to Auschwitz." This point was further highlighted by Oxford literature professor and poet Tom Paulin who told the Egyptian newspaper *Al-Ahram* that American Jewish settlers on the West Bank and Gaza were "Nazis" who should be "shot dead."

In Germany, a public controversy broke out when Jamal Karsli, a Syrian-born member of parliament, who had to leave the Green Party after he claimed that Israel was using "Nazi methods" against the Palestinians and criticized the influence of the "Zionist lobby" in Germany, was welcomed with open arms into the FDP (Free Democratic Party—the Liberals) by deputy chairman Jürgen Möllemann, himself a harsh critic of Israel and head of the German-Arab Friendship Association. In the course of the public debate that followed, Josef Joffe, editor of the prestigious weekly *Die Zeit* commented: "Recent events are more than breaking a taboo on antisemitic expressions; they are uprooting the most basic ethos of postwar Germany: the consensus which determined that this is a liberal democracy, without racism or antisemitism." After the general elections, on 22 November 2002, when it became clear that Möllemann's antisemitic statements had contributed to the defeat of the conservative-liberal coalition, Möllemann was forced to resign as deputy head of the FDP. On 17 March he resigned from the party, retaining, however, his seat in the Bundestag. . . .

Antisemitism in the United States

Like western Europe, in the US, too, some anti-war groups incorporated extreme anti-Israel and sometimes antisemitic expressions in their protests against the impending campaign against Iraq. The ANSWER (Act Now to Stop War and End

Racism) coalition, created by the New York–based International Action Center to protest the bombing of Afghanistan, has organized many anti-war protests around the country since September 2001. Anti-Israel and antisemitic content has marked some ANSWER events, which have been endorsed by such groups as the international Al-Awda–Right of Return Coalition and the Illinois-based Islamic Association for Palestine (IAP).

> *In the minds of those who adhere to antisemitic conspiracy theories, anti-Americanism and antisemitism have become inseparable.*

ANSWER has become one of the most effective organizers of anti-war rallies, playing a key role in bringing Arab and Muslim groups into the anti-war and anti-racism movements, which has led to extreme invective against Israel during protests. The largest and most disturbing ANSWER event was held on 20 April 2002, in Washington, DC. Called the "National March for Palestine against War and Racism," the rally was attended by approximately 200,000 people, including thousands of pro-Palestinian demonstrators. The rally served as a forum for supporting violence and terror organizations, and for a proliferation of antisemitic expressions. Slogans and images included: "End the Holocaust" (with a picture of [Israeli prime minister, Ariel] Sharon), an Israeli flag with a swastika replacing the Star of David, a US flag with a Star of David replacing the 50 stars and the message, "Free America," "Bush and Sharon, Tag-team Terrorists," and "First Jesus Now Arafat, Stop the Killers." The ANSWER coalition advanced the date of its rally to April 20 to coincide with anti-globalization demonstrations, which were organized to protest the IMF [International Monetary Fund] and the World Bank. . . .

Antisemitism in Latin America

A general increase in antisemitism has been discerned in Latin America, noticeably in comparisons between Israeli conduct in the territories and Hitler's actions in World War II—verbally, in images and at demonstrations. As elsewhere, Israel's policy in the territories became an important lever for some groups which once showed no signs of antisemitism to make the symbolic comparisons between Israel and Nazi Germany, Sharon and Hitler, the Star of David and the swastika. In 2002, these expressions became far more common in the media and television, in protest demonstrations, on posters and in graffiti.

In Brazil, extreme anti-Israel sentiments were voiced both by students and faculty in universities. In every public debate Sharon was compared to Hitler. The claim that Jews and Israel were the driving force behind the American campaigns, together with shrill anti-Israel remarks, appeared in the Brazilian media and at protest rallies. The leftist magazine *Liberacion* published a virulently antisemitic editorial entitled "Israeli Nazi Methods," which compared Israel's actions in the territories to those of the Nazis in World War II. Antisemitic caricatures have appeared repeatedly in Brazil. On 14 April 2002, *Correio Brazilliense* published a caricature showing the devil sitting at a table with a flag bearing the Star of David behind him. A caricature in *O Globo* in April [2003] showed Sharon wearing a blood-soaked apron, grasping a knife shaped like an Israeli flag with which he is butchering Arabs on the table before him. . . .

Swastikas and antisemitic slogans were drawn on the Israeli embassy in Mexico City. Anti-Zionist and anti-Israel demonstrations held in Mexico on 3 and 4 April [2003] were also antisemitic. Among the organizers were members of the guerilla organization active in Mexico during the last years, the Zapatista Army National Liberation (EZLN), founded in the Chiapas area to promote a land redemption scheme for members of the army. The fact that this once purely local action group participated in an anti-Israel and anti-Zionist demonstration demonstrates that it is making inroads amongst leftists nationwide. . . .

Antisemitism and Anti-Americanism

Antisemitism, a central element of extreme right ideology, has been observed increasingly in the rhetoric of all shades of the left. A vital influence on this development in many countries has been the antisemitic/anti-Zionist argumentation of radical Islamists, in the form of anti-Americanism. In the minds of those who adhere to antisemitic conspiracy theories, anti-Americanism and antisemitism have become inseparable.

Millions throughout the world demonstrated their opposition to the potential attack on the Baghdad regime. United by strong anti-globalization and anti-American feelings, people of conflicting political views marched together. In Europe in particular, the extreme right depicts America as the symbol of racial impurity and plutocracy ruled by the "all-powerful Jews," while the communists and the Marxist left, characterize the US as the homeland of capitalism and imperialism.

In scapegoating Israel and the Jews the speed and apparent authenticity of the Internet has played a major role. One example was the tragic fate of the US space shuttle. According to one rumor, the disaster was caused intentionally by the Jews and Israelis to distract world attention from events in the Middle East. Another conspiracy theory accused Israeli astronaut Ilan Ramon of having been on a secret spy mission against Iraq. . . .

The Influence of American Jews on US Policy

Since the fall of 2002, public remarks about the Iraq crisis have increasingly implicated Israel and American Jews. While most observers remain fair-minded in assessing the many other factors that influence US policy, some have stated or implied that Israel, and high-ranking American Jews in the Bush administration, are pushing the US into war—forcing it against its own interests to undertake what has variously been called "Israel's war" and "a war for the Jews." These accusations were raised by both conservatives and right-wingers as well as by leftists. They appeared not only in extreme right and extreme left publications, but in various mainstream ones, too. It should be noted that prior to the American attack, a poll by the Pew Research Center for the People and the Press found that while 62 percent of all Americans supported the war, only 52 percent of the Jews did. . . .

While in mainstream papers the Jewish origin of "neo-conservatives" who allegedly pushed America into war was only insinuated, it was openly expressed by well known antisemites such as leading American white supremacist and a former leader of the Ku Klux Klan David Duke, in his Online Radio Report (5 March 2003) under the title: "No War for Israel!" Duke wrote:

> By any standard, this Iraq war is of no benefit to the United States of America, nor is it of any benefit to the commercial oil industry. So, for whose benefit does America wage this war? The answer is Israel. Israel, Israel! Radical Jewish supremacists in Israel launched this drive for war. Their agents all

over the world, both in government and media, have been the real power behind this war. . . .

It is my hope that for the sake of our brave, young fighting men, and indeed, for the people of our nation, that by a miracle we can avoid this Jewish war.

A similar statement was made by Louis Farrakhan, head of the Nation of Islam in a Savior's Day speech, in Chicago (23 February 2003):

The warmongers in his [President Bush's] administration, the poor Israeli Zionists, have literally gotten America's foreign policy to protect Israel. Now many of you won't say these things, but that's on you. [The late journalist] Daniel Pearl or [conservative political adviser] Richard Perle, [Deputy Secretary of Defense Paul] Wolfowitz, [conservative columnist William] Kristol—all of these are architects of policy and they are pro-Israel. One American congressman said, "Listen, the cornerstone of America's foreign policy is the protection of Israel.". . .

Anti-Americanism and Antisemitism in the Arab World

In his national address on state television on 24 March 2003, as the US-led invasion to overthrow him went into its fifth day, Iraqi President Saddam Husayn attacked "the intentions and goals of the American and British administrations, which are driven by accursed Zionism." At a televised Friday sermon broadcast about a month and half earlier at a mosque in Baghdad, Shaykh Bakr Samara'i theatrically drew a sword from a sheath and waved it angrily in the air, warning America and Britain of God's wrath and blaming the Jews, "descendants of apes and pigs," of plotting and inflaming internecine wars on earth through the ages by using their money and the media. This perception of the Jews/Zionists/Israelis as plotters who were behind all the alleged malaise inflicted on Arabs and Muslims was the dominant antisemitic theme in the Arab discourse on major regional and international issues throughout the year. . . .

Palestinian journalist Khalid 'Amayrah claimed in an article, published by the Islamic Association for Palestine (IAP) site on

27 November 2002, that "Zionists and their supporters" should not be surprised about the proliferation of antisemitism among Arabs and Muslims. Jews, he asserted, vilify Muslims, Arabs and the Palestinian people in the West, and harbor "Nazi-like designs on the utterly defenseless Palestinian people."

The theme of the alleged Jewish anti-Muslim and anti-Arab drive emanated also from the representation of the September 11 events. The canard that the Jews were behind the attacks on the World Trade Center and the Pentagon continued unabated among the Arab and Muslim public as well as among journalists and commentators. A Gallup Poll conducted in nine Muslim countries (Pakistan, Iran, Indonesia, Turkey, Lebanon, Morocco, Kuwait, Jordan and Saudi Arabia) found that the majority of the population in these countries (61 percent)—with the exception of the West-aligned Turkey, with only 43 percent—refused to believe that Arabs had carried out the bombings. They believed without any doubt that it was a Mossad [Israeli secret police] conspiracy; even those who attributed the bombings to al-Qa'ida members thought that they were Mossad operators who had successfully infiltrated the organization.

On the eve of the war, during February and March [2003], prominent Muslim clerics including Shaykh al-Azhar Muhammad Sayyid al-Tantawi and Yusuf al-Qaradawi issued edicts (*fatwas*), calling on Arabs and Muslims to launch a holy war (jihad) to defend themselves against the US invasion. They described the military buildup in the Persian Gulf as a new crusade, and hence according to Islamic law, "if the enemy steps on Muslims' land, jihad becomes a duty incumbent upon every Muslim male and female." In an article posted on the movement's website in January [2003], Palestinian [terrorist group] Hamas spokesman 'Abd al-'Aziz al-Rantisi called on Iraq to use the tactics of Islamist jihad warriors and establish a suicide army composed of Muslim volunteers to halt the Crusader aggression.

It should be noted, however, that Arab commentaries also included harsh criticism of Saddam. He was blamed for bringing war upon himself by his policies, disregarding the damage to his own people. Moreover, some writers even dared to suggest that he resign and seek political asylum in an Arab country—a proposal officially adopted by Arab leaders who sought to avoid a disaster in Iraq and feared that the war would shake up the Middle East and give rise to extremism.

2

The Revival of Abandoned Christian Doctrine Encourages Anti-Semitism

Melanie Phillips

Melanie Phillips, a political columnist for the British news-paper the Daily Mail, *has written social and political com-mentary for other British papers, including the* Observer *and the* Sunday Times. *Awarded the Orwell Prize for jour-nalism in 1996, she is also the author of* All Must Have Prizes, *a study of the British educational crisis.*

In some Christian churches, the doctrine of replace-ment theology is reviving anti-Semitism. According to this doctrine, the Christians have replaced the Jews in God's favor. Therefore, all God's promises to the Jews, including the right to the land of Israel, have been in-herited by Christianity. Many Christian leaders have thus tried to repudiate Jewish claims to the land of Is-rael. Anti-Israel statements by some clergy have influ-enced some church members to develop anti-Semitic feelings. Although some church leaders have spoken out against replacement theology and anti-Semitism, prejudice and fear of Jews still runs deep in many Chris-tian churches.

It was one of those sickening moments when an illusion is shattered and an ominous reality laid bare. I was among a group of Jews and Christians who met recently to discuss the churches' increasing public hostility to Israel. The Jews were braced for a difficult encounter. After all, many British Jews (of whom I am one) are themselves appalled by the destruction of Palestinian villages, targeted assassinations and other apparent Israeli over-reactions to the middle east conflict.

But this debate never took place. For the Christians said that the churches' hostility had nothing to do with Israel's behaviour towards the Palestinians. This was merely an excuse. The real reason for the growing antipathy, according to the Christians at that meeting, was the ancient hatred of Jews rooted deep inside Christian theology and now on widespread display once again.

The Revival of Replacement Theology

A doctrine going back to the early church fathers, suppressed after the Holocaust, had been revived under the influence of the middle east conflict. This doctrine is called replacement theology. In essence, this says the Jews have been replaced by the Christians in God's favour and so all God's promises to the Jews, including the land of Israel, have been inherited by Christianity.

Some evangelicals, by contrast, are 'Christian Zionists' who passionately support the State of Israel as the fulfilment of God's Biblical promise to the Jews. But to the majority who have absorbed replacement theology, Zionism [movement to support the Jewish state of Israel] is racism and the Jewish state is illegitimate.

The Jews at the meeting were incredulous and aghast. Surely the Christians were exaggerating. Surely the churches' dislike of Israel was rooted instead in the settlements, the occupied territories and Prime Minister Ariel Sharon. But the Christians were adamant. The hostility to Israel within the church is rooted in a dislike of the Jews.

Church newspaper editors say they are intimidated by the overwhelming hostility to Israel and to the Jews from influential Christian figures, which makes balanced coverage of the middle east impossible. Clerics and lay people alike are saying openly that Israel should never have been founded at all. One church source said what he was hearing was a 'throwback to the visceral anti-Judaism of the middle ages'.

At this juncture, a distinction is crucial. Criticism of Israel's behaviour is perfectly legitimate. But a number of prominent

Christians agree that a line is being crossed into anti-Jewish hatred. This is manifested by ascribing to every Israeli action malevolent motives while dismissing Palestinian terrorism and anti-Jewish diatribes; the belief that Jews should be denied the right to self-determination and their state dismantled; the conflation of Zionism and a 'Jewish conspiracy' of vested interests; and the disproportionate venom of the attacks.

> *To the majority who have absorbed replacement theology, Zionism is racism and the Jewish state is illegitimate.*

'When I hear "the Jews" used as a term, my blood runs cold—and I've been hearing this far too often', says Rowan Williams, Archbishop of Wales and a contender for the see of Canterbury. 'Whenever I print anything sympathetic to Israel, I get deluged with complaints that I am Zionist and racist', says Colin Blakely, editor of the *Church of England* newspaper.

Andrew White, canon of Coventry cathedral and the Archbishop of Canterbury's representative in the Middle East, is heavily engaged in trying to promote dialogue and peace between Israelis and Palestinians. He says of attitudes in the church: 'These go beyond legitimate criticism of Israel into hatred of the Jews. I get hate mail calling me a Jew-lover and saying my work is evil'.

The reason, he says, is that Palestinian Christian revisionism has revived replacement theology. 'This doctrine was key in fanning the flames of the Holocaust, which could not have happened without 2,000 years of anti-Jewish polemic', he says. After the Holocaust the Vatican officially buried the doctrine, the current Pope affirming the integrity of the Jewish people and recognising the State of Israel. But according to White, the doctrine is 'still vibrant' within Roman Catholic and Anglican pews. 'Almost all the churches hold to replacement theology', he says.

Arab Christians Attack Israel

The catalyst for its re-emergence has been the attempt by Arab Christians to reinterpret Scripture in order to de-legitimise the Jews' claim to the land of Israel. This has had a powerful effect upon the churches which, through humanitarian work among the Palestinians by agencies like Christian Aid, have been profoundly influenced by two clerics in particular.

The first is the Anglican Bishop of Jerusalem, Riah Abu El-Assal, a Palestinian who is intemperate in his attacks on Israel. 'We interviewed Bishop Riah after some terrorist outrage in Israel', says Colin Blakely, 'and his line was that it was all the fault of the Jews. I was astounded'.

The bishop also has an astounding interpretation of the Old Testament. [In] December [2001], he claimed of Palestinian Christians: 'We are the true Israel . . . no-one can deny me the right to inherit the promises, and after all the promises were first given to Abraham and Abraham is never spoken of in the Bible as a Jew. . . . He is the father of the faithful'.

The second cleric, Father Naim Ateek, is more subtle and highly influential. Although he says he has come to accept Israel's existence, his brand of radical liberation theology undermines it by attempting to sever the special link between God and the Jews.

In a lecture [in 2001], Andrew White observed that Palestinian politics and Christian theology had become inextricably intertwined. The Palestinians were viewed as oppressed and the church had to fight their oppressor. 'Who is their oppressor? The state of Israel. Who is Israel? The Jews. It is they therefore who must be put under pressure so that the oppressed may one day be set free to enter their "Promised Land" which is being denied to them'.

> *This doctrine [replacement theology] was key in fanning the flames of the Holocaust, which could not have happened without 2,000 years of anti-Jewish polemic.*

This view, said White, had now influenced not only whole denominations but the majority of Christian pilgrimage companies and many of the major mission and Christian aid organisations. One such outfit, he said, had sent every UK bishop a significant document outlining Israel's oppression of the Palestinians, accusing Israel of ethnic cleansing and of systematically 'Judaising' Jerusalem.

David Ison, the canon of Exeter cathedral, took a party of pilgrims to the Holy Land in 2000 at the start of the current intifada. They had a Palestinian guide, visited only Christian sites in Arab east Jerusalem and the West Bank, and talked to virtually no Jews. 'The Old Testament is a horrifying picture of genocide committed in God's name', he avers. 'And genocide is now being waged in a long, slow way by Zionists against the Palestinians'.

Asked what he made of [leader of the Palestine Liberation Organization] Yasser Arafat's rejection of the offers made by Israel at Camp David and Tabah [peace conferences] he said he knew nothing about that. Indeed, he said, he knew nothing about Israel beyond what he had read in a book by an advocate of replacement theology, with which he agreed, and what he had been told by the Palestinians on the pilgrimage.

British Church Officials Condemn Israel

The Bishop of Guildford [in the United Kingdom] who is consistently hostile to Israel, shares the view that the Jews have no particular claim to the promised land. Christianity and Islam, he says, can lay equal claim. And although he says Israel's existence is a reality that must be accepted, his ideal is very different. A separate Palestinian state would be merely a 'first step'.

'Ultimately, one shared land is the vision one would want to pursue, although it's unlikely this will come about'. As for the churches' hostility to Israel, his reply is chilling. 'The problem is that all the power lies with the Israeli state'. So by implication, Israel would only merit sympathy for its casualties if it had no power to defend itself.

The Bishop of Guildford, who chairs Christian Aid, says he particularly admires Bishop Riah and Naim Ateek. He also warmly endorses a parish priest in his diocese: Stephen Sizer, vicar of Christ Church, Virginia Water.

Sizer is a leading crusader against Christian Zionism. He believes that God's promises to the Jews have been inherited by Christianity, including the land of Israel. 'A return to Jewish nationalism', he has written, 'would seem incompatible with this New Testament perspective of the international community of Jesus'.

He acknowledges that Israel has the right to exist since it was established by a United Nations resolution. But he also says it is 'fundamentally an apartheid [racially segregated] state because it is based on race', and 'even worse than South Africa' (this despite the fact that Israeli Arabs have the vote, they are members of the Knesset [Israel's legislature] and one is even a Supreme Court judge).

He therefore hopes Israel will go the same way as South Africa under apartheid, 'brought to an end internally by the rising up of the people'. So despite saying he supports Israel's existence, he appears to want the Jewish state to be singled out for a fate afforded to no other democracy properly constituted under international law.

But perhaps this is not surprising given his attitude towards Jews. 'The covenant between Jews and God', he states, 'was conditional on their respect for human rights. The reason they were expelled from the land was that they were more interested in money and power and treated the poor and aliens with contempt'. Today's Jews, it appears, are no better. 'In the United States, politicians dare not criticise Israel because half the funding for both the Democrats and the Republicans comes from Jewish sources'.

A Dislike of the Jews

A number of authoritative Christian figures are extremely concerned by the elision between criticism of Israel and dislike of the Jews. Rowan Williams says that after a website of the Church in Wales attracted inflammatory language about Jews, and a meeting in Cardiff [Wales] about Israel provoked similar anti-Jewish rhetoric, he was forced to introduce some balancing material about the middle east into his church periodicals.

Dr Patrick Sookhdeo, director of the Institute for the Study of Islam and Christianity, has been addressing Christian groups up and down the country on the implications of [the terrorist attacks of] 11 September [2001]. When he suggests there is a problem with aspects of Islam, he provokes uproar. His audiences blame Israel for Muslim anger; they want to abandon the Jewish state as a 'dead' part of Scripture and support 'justice' for the Palestinians instead. 'What disturbs me at the moment is the very deeply-rooted anti-semitism latent in Britain and the west', he says. 'I simply hadn't realised how deep within the English psyche is this fear of the power and influence of the Jews'.

Since 11 September, he says, the Palestinian issue has had a major distorting impact on the whole of the Christian world. 'Those who blame Israel for everything don't realise that for Islam, the very existence of Israel is a problem. Even a Palestinian state would not be sufficient. Israel may be behaving illegally in a number of areas, but she is under attack. But white liberal Christians find it deeply offensive not to blame Israel for injustice'.

The Archbishop of Canterbury, George Carey [leader of Church of England], has spoken out against replacement theology. But unlike the Roman Catholics, the Anglicans have never been forced to confront their church's role in the Holocaust and their attitude towards the Jews.

Carey, say church sources, is now in an invidious position. Under pressure to make an accommodation with the Muslims, he is also hemmed in by some highly placed enemies of Israel within the church and is reluctant to pick a fight with the establishment view.

Nevertheless, there are many decent Christians who don't hold this view. The network of councils of Christians and Jews is going strong. Archbishop Williams [has] preached in Cardiff's synagogue. . . . Christians who voice these concerns are prepared to risk opprobrium or worse.

But for the Jews, caught between the Islamists' blood libels [accusations of Jewish ritual murder] on one side and Christian replacement theology on the other, Britain is suddenly a colder place.

3

Christian Principles Reject Anti-Semitism

David R. Mason

David R. Mason, a priest associate at St. Paul's Episcopal Church in Cleveland, Ohio, is also a professor in the Department of Religious Studies at John Carroll University in Cleveland.

In the New Testament Gospels, the Jews are held responsible for persecuting Jesus, despite the fact that his execution was ordered by Pilate, the Roman governor. It is particularly in the Gospel of John that the root of much Christian anti-Semitism can be found. In this Gospel, Jesus is not only in conflict with the policies and philosophies of the Jewish scribes, Pharisees, and other Jewish leaders, but is pitted against the Jewish people as a whole. This conflict in the Gospels reflects the historic tensions between early Christians and Jews in the first century A.D. Despite the conflicts between Christians and Jews, the first principle of Christian belief is in God's love for everyone. Jesus showed his love (and God's love) for all humankind when he sacrificed himself on the cross. Belief in a God who loves all people means embracing and cherishing the freedom and the values of others. Thus, for someone who is a Christian, there is no place for racism or anti-Semitism in their religious beliefs.

The first and most obvious point to make about racism generally and about the specific form it takes in one's prejudicial attitudes and behavior toward African-Americans and Jews is that it is simply wrong: It is harmful, poisonous, and sinful.

David R. Mason, "A Christian Alternative to (Christian) Racism and Antisemitism," *Journal of Ecumenical Studies*, vol. 37, Spring 2000, p. 151. Copyright © 2000 by *Journal of Ecumenical Studies*. Reproduced by permission.

Caricatures and stereotyping derived from ignorance bred from fear of that which is different (xenophobia), the perpetuation of language that reinforces negative attitudes, half-truths and out-and-out lies, and the erection of and participation in social, economic, and political structures that exclude individuals from realizing their fullest potential because of membership in a group, even where it is not clearly illegal—are all immoral. . . .

Therefore, when I reflect on the difficulty of providing sound practical solutions to the problems of entrenched and frequently institutionalized racism, I become increasingly convinced of the necessity to return to first principles for critical examination. . . .

The fundamental principles that I would have us examine as a basis for reordering human relations equably are Christian principles. I recognize that an appeal to Christian principles might appear to be exclusivist or even triumphalist [superior to all other religions] rather than productive of multicultural comity. Insofar as Christian claims have been exclusivist or triumphalist, they are part of the problem rather than the solution. I believe, and will argue, that fundamental Christian principles are neither and that, as representative of authentic human values, Christian principles must give voice to these fruits of authentic human faith: freedom, justice, and good will toward all. Further, to say that they are Christian principles does not preclude their lying at the heart of other religions as well. . . .

> *There can be little doubt that the Holocaust of the Jews in the 1930's and 1940's is, at least partially, the direct result of 2,000 years of Christian anti-Judaism.*

The chief victims of racism in America, African-Americans, originally created their own culture out of the diverse memories of an African past, the common experience of slavery, and the Christianity taught them by white slaveowners. No matter that the white masters may have tried to inculcate such biblical passages as "Slaves, accept the authority of your masters" (1 Pet. 2:18), black slaves quickly learned to interpret their own experience and to formulate their destiny in terms of the Exodus of Hebrew slaves from Egypt, the prophetic demand for justice, and above all the story of Jesus. However much the black experience in America has been shaped by its African heritage and by slavery and continued racial prejudice and institutionalized discrimination, it has been nurtured on biblical religion, tutored by Christian ideas, and given hope by Christian ideals. These have sustained many African-Americans through considerable suffering at the hands of white Christians.

Anti-Semitism in the Gospels

If there is a case for linking American culture generally, and African-American culture specifically, to Christian values, this is not as apparent for Jews and Christians. There can be no doubt that the history of Christian-Jewish relations is the history of calumny, slurs, negative stereotypes, segregation, and oppression. There can be little doubt that the Holocaust of the Jews in the 1930's and 1940's is, at least partially, the direct result of 2,000 years of Christian anti-Judaism. Moreover, honesty demands that the root of much Christian anti-Jewish slander be located in the Second Testament itself, especially the Gospels. . . .

The hostility between Jesus and the Jewish leaders is brought to a head with the death of Jesus. Although all four Gospels agree that his execution was by crucifixion—clearly a Roman execution—they also portray the Roman official Pilate as but the innocent stooge of the Jewish high priests and the Sanhedrin, finally bending to the wish of the Jewish people to crucify him. "Thus," as . . . scholar [Michael Cook] put it, "paradoxically did a Jew put to death by the Romans become, instead, a Christian put to death by Jews."

If the "Synoptic Gospels" (Matthew, Mark, Luke) typically only portray the Jewish leaders as the enemies of Jesus, responsible for his death, the Gospel of John paints a clear and vivid picture of "the Jews" as a group as being vicious adversaries of Jesus. Here it is "the Jews," not merely the Pharisees or the high priests or even "the people" who are thus vilified. The term, "the Jews," is used seventy-one times in John, as opposed to a total of sixteen times in the other three Gospels together. Moreover, at least twenty-five of the usages are plainly negative, even hostile; for example, Jn. 5:16 and 5:18: "Therefore the Jews started persecuting Jesus" and "For this reason the Jews were seeking all the more to kill him," culminating with 19:14–15: "the Jews . . . cried out, 'Away with him! Away with him! Crucify him.'". . .

Any Christian who is not profoundly disturbed, even shaken, by the virulent anti-Jewishness of this Gospel should, at the very least, try the experiment of reading it as if he or she were a Jew—one whose people have been persecuted at the hands of Christians down through the centuries. I have tried this and have concluded that the remark of a rabbi [Kaufmann Kolder] in 1905 rings true: that John is the "gospel of Christian love and Jew[ish] hatred." This is all the more troubling because John has been the most popular of Christian writings, readily translated, and the source of many easily memorized passages. Indeed, it contains much that is spiritually and theologically profound. Unfortunately, the effect of all this has been to suggest that the anti-Jewishness that pervades it is part-and-parcel of the gospel of God's universal redemptive love rather than what it is: a historical aberration rooted in the unusually bitter Christian-Jewish relations of the late first century.

Are there good reasons for believing that the anti-Jewish sentiment so plainly evident in the Gospel of John, but also a part of the other Gospels, is far from, even at odds with, the fundamental principle of the Christian message? There are.

The Gospels Are Theology, Not History

It has long been clear to Second Testament scholars, even if this has not been made clear to the public at large, that none of the Gospels is an eyewitness account of the historical Jesus. Nor are the Gospels an attempt to record the biography of Jesus. All were written in the last third of the first century, and all the Gospel writers were editors, not reporters. They were people who fashioned quite different accounts from stories and sayings that circulated for several generations among the earliest Christian communities. Some of the sayings circulated without any narrative framework, while other sayings and stories were found embedded in liturgies, preaching, and controversies with local Jewish congregations. The Gospel writers synthesized these diverse stories and sayings into a new whole, creating sequences and situations, and even placing words in Jesus' mouth. John is the most highly theological and the least historically reliable, but all the Gospels must be regarded as narrative theology rather than biographical record. Inevitably, all of them reflect the times and situations in which they were written. . . .

Whether, or to what extent, anyone can penetrate the layers to attempt to form an accurate picture of the historical Jesus is still very much in debate. What is certain, though, is that whatever emerges will be fragmentary: perhaps a teacher and healer who proclaimed the imminence of God's reign and associated himself with its advent, a Jew who gathered disciples and was put to death by the Roman government.

The important thing, however, is that all the above is proclaimed throughout the Second Testament. . . . That is to say, the disciples and others quickly became convinced that death had not crushed Jesus and that somehow he was among them. Thus they, and the generations following them who produced the Second Testament, found their own lives quickened and oriented anew toward the only God they knew how to believe in— the God of Abraham, Isaac, and Jacob, the God of Moses and the prophets, the Redeemer of Israel and the Creator of the universe. Now, however, they were enabled to see God through the lens of Jesus. For this group Jesus decisively re-presented ultimate reality and the meaning of authentic existence for them.

It is important to note the use of the term, "re-presents," which I have borrowed from theologian Schubert Ogden, who has used it to make the same point that I wish to make: Contrary to any exclusivist or triumphalist claim for Jesus as the sole locus of divine activity in the world—a claim that on the face of it is as immoral as it is absurd—the essential witness to Jesus in the Second Testament is a witness to one who for the apostolic community dramatically and decisively presents anew the pure unbounded love of the God who is always already present to every creature, not only as its creative ground but also as the redemptive love that will never abandon it. Thus, Jesus is taken to be representative of, but not alone constitutive of, the divine redemptive love that alone saves or justifies any human being.

The Fundamental Christian Principle

This view maintains that the ultimate reality that is internally related to every creature as its creative source and the ultimate recipient of all its acts—its Whence and its Whither—is none other than the loving God known to the Jews decisively as their liberator from slavery in Egypt, as the source of Torah that orders the life of Israel, as the One whose steadfast love proclaimed by the prophets chastens Israel but will not let it go. This God is also the One who is there at creation and breathes spirit into humans and, so, is disclosed as the God of the nations as well as of Israel; ultimately, this is the God of hope.

This same God is known to Christians decisively in Jesus. Here the major Jewish themes of liberation, law, call to repentance, creation, and hope are re-presented, and all focus on the cross as the symbol of divine suffering love. God is here attested as "the great companion, the fellow-sufferer who understands," [writes philosopher] Alfred North Whitehead. The point should be made that the crucifixion is taken neither merely as a tragic historical event nor as a divine bolt out the blue; it is the symbol of universal divine love. . . .

If this goes to the heart of the Christian proclamation, any sort of exclusivism or ethnocentrism is ruled out as antithetical to the first principles of the Christian witness of faith. Just as Jews know themselves to have been "chosen"—not for special favors but to bear witness to all the world, often through their suffering, to God's steadfast love and justice—so Christians are called to bear witness to this same God's redemptive love for every creature in the world. The point of the Christian faith in Jesus as "re-presentative" of God is not to get people to join a particular religion in order to be saved but to witness to the conviction that God is creatively and redemptively at work in the lives of all people, irrespective of their cultural identity, their religion, or their political or socioeconomic status. . . .

No One True Religion

There is no evidence that there is but one true religion—much less a superior ethnic group—such that anyone wishing to share God's redemptive love must be initiated into that religion or be born into that ethnic group. There is every reason to reject this as opposed not only to common sense and the ethics of toleration but also to the deepest principles of faith in God. Nor is there any evidence that the earliest Christians thought they constituted such an absolutely true religion. From the beginning, the greatest apostles of faith have directed human trust and commitment toward God rather than toward some decisive nationality, one exclusive sect, or one set of beliefs and rules. This, it seems evident, is the point of Paul's discovery that salvation lies not in works of the Law but in faith in God. . . .

Thus, Paul urged the believers in Galatia not to sink back into sectarianism: "There is no longer Jew or Greek, there is no longer slave or free, there is no longer male and female; for all of you are one in Christ Jesus" (Gal. 3:28). Similarly, Paul, or a disciple of his, told the Colossians: "In that renewal there is no longer Greek and Jew, circumcised and uncircumcised, barbarian, Scythian, slave and free; but Christ is all and in all!" (Col. 3:11). "Christ" in both cases is not intended in a narrow, sectarian sense, but as the God "represented" by Jesus. . . .

> **// *An examination of the fundamental Christian vision . . . shows that the demons of anti-Semitism and racism should be banished from Christian self-understanding.* //**

I have labored this point because it is so easily distorted or twisted into its opposite. Christianity in particular, as practiced through the ages, can almost be read as the triumph of the negative image. Yet, despite the constant human tendency to reduce the divine to something familiar and manageable or, in [theologian Reinhold] Niebuhr's words, to "absolutize the relative," the fundamental message remains: That which anchors all human existence, that which is the ground of all meaning and value, is nothing as contingent as a particular religion or an ethnic identity but only that to which all religions point, the circumambiant reality that is the source and goal of all finite beings, the One "in whom we live and move and have our being." It is what theistic religions symbolize as "Yahweh," "God: Father, Son, and Holy Spirit," and "Allah"; others as "Brahman," "Nirvana," "the Tao," etc. Implicitly, it is that about the world that gives to every being the sense that it is "something that matters" [as] Alfred North Whitehead [wrote].

To be authentically human—human in the best way possible rather than as having fallen prey to superstition, idolatry, bigotry, pride, despair, etc.—is to place one's trust utterly in this transcendent, yet universally present, reality. Such trust is what Paul called "faith." Call it what you will, but do not confuse it with excessive zeal misdirected toward some human institution or set of ideas. Such zeal is idolatry and is the counterfeit of faith. . . .

The genuine article demands that people face their own lives and histories and the world around them honestly and with eyes wide open: "You will know the truth, and the truth will make you free" (Jn. 8:32).

Such faith is an orientation of the whole person that undergirds intellect, emotion, and will and gives these elements of personality purpose; it places what a person does in this life, and how it is done, in a larger context. Perhaps the finest religious expression of this attitude is the summary of the Jewish religion as expressed by Jesus: "'You shall love the Lord your God with all your heart, and with all your soul, and with all your mind.' This is the greatest and first commandment. And a second is like it: 'You shall love your neighbor as yourself.' On these two commandments hang all the law and the prophets" (Mt. 22:37–40, synthesizing Dt. 6:5 and Lev. 19:18). This expression of the basic attitude or orientation indicates that one's final trust must not be placed in anything finite (which would be idolatry, giving rise to furious zeal) but only in that which abides. It also makes clear that this orientation is essentially love: love that integrates intellect, emotion, and will, with the totality of one's being. . . .

Freedom from Racism

Even so, as has been well said [by Schubert Ogden], "the one test of whether love is really present is always freedom." Or, as Paul said, "Where the Spirit of the Lord is, there is freedom" (2 Cor. 3:17). Again, speaking sharply to those in Galatia who had allowed themselves to be enslaved to a certain kind of religiosity, he said: "For freedom Christ has set us free. Stand firm, therefore, and do not submit again to a yoke of slavery" (Gal. 5:1). . . .

There are many things that oppress or enslave people. Not only are persons physically and mentally limited, but they are often slaves to their own prejudicial and narrow-minded views, prisoners to an ideology, oppressed by past decisions and anxieties about creaturely transience and the fear that one will make no difference in the world. Beyond the things for which anyone might be personally responsible there are powerful social attitudes that have been inherited, political and economic structures that both support and are supported by particular individuals. To exist faithfully in freedom is not to eliminate any of these factors that help to frame human, historical existence, but it is to keep them in perspective so that they are never the final arbiters of one's existence.

In terms of the issues on which I have focused, to rely upon that which transcends all finite, historical relativities is to be liberated from the idolatry that insists that my religion or my particular set of ethnic values is the ultimate standard by which all truth, beauty, and goodness are to be judged. As such, faith is the beginning of freedom from any sort of religious exclusivism, triumphalism, racism, or ethnocentrism.

Moreover, after being liberated from such oppressors, one is bound to seek to optimize the limits of others' freedom. This work has already begun when one changes one's attitude, when one recognizes that one's own way is not the only way or the only right way, when one is able to celebrate the richness of diverse cultures and religions and to gain the confidence that an encompassing whole can embrace and cherish the values of all. The work of optimizing others' freedom requires changing structures as well as attitudes, changing habits of buying, investing, living, valuing; it demands that persons be proactive in diminishing remarks, habits, and structures that demean, degrade, misrepresent, suppress, or physically harm others.

Such demons abound in our society. There is much that cries out for freedom. A return to fundamental principles, an examination of the fundamental Christian vision, however, shows that the demons of anti-Semitism and racism should be banished from Christian self-understanding.

4

The Policies of Some Israeli Leaders Concerning Palestinians Provoke Anti-Semitism

Uri Avnery

Uri Avnery, a founding member of Gush Shalom, the Israeli peace party, was a Zionist independence fighter in Palestine and later a soldier in the Israeli army. He served in the Israeli parliament, the Knesset, and was the first Israeli to make contact with the Palestine Liberation Organization (PLO) in 1974. He was also the first Israeli to meet with PLO leader Yasir Arafat, in 1982 during the war in Lebanon. A journalist and author, he has written a number of books on the Palestinian/Israeli conflict and has served as editor in chief of the newsmagazine Ha'olam Haze *for more than forty years.*

Because of Prime Minister Ariel Sharon's policies against the Palestinians, Israel, once seen as a haven for an oppressed people who were defending themselves against assaults by murderous Arabs, is now seen by the world as the oppressor of a weak, defenseless Palestinian people. The image of Israel as a militaristic aggressor has created opposition to Israel's policies across the globe, thus helping hard-core anti-Semites win others to their racist cause. Jews throughout the world should not blindly defend the policies of Israel's government. The most effective way to disarm the anti-Semites is to speak out against unfair and inhuman treatment of the Palestinians.

The first Israeli victim of [former Iraqi dictator] Saddam Hussein is a Zionist myth on which we were brought up.

The myth tells us that Israel is a haven for all the Jews in the world. In all the other countries, we are told, Jews live in perpetual fear that a cruel persecutor will arise, as happened in Germany. Israel is the safe haven, to which Jews can escape in times of danger. Indeed, this was the purpose of Israel's founding fathers when they established the state.

Now Saddam comes along and proves the opposite. All over the world, Jews live in safety; they are threatened by annihilation in only one place on the planet: Israel. Here national parks are being prepared for use as mass graves, here (pathetic) measures against biological and chemical weapons are being prepared. Many people are already planning to escape to the communities in the Diaspora. End of a myth.

Another Zionist myth died even before that: The Diaspora, so we learned in our youth, creates anti-Semitism. Everywhere the Jews are a minority, and a minority inevitably attracts the hatred of the majority. Only when the Jews gather in the land of their forefathers and constitute the majority there, we learned, will anti-Semitism disappear throughout the world. Thus spoke [Theodor] Herzl, the founder of modern Zionism.

Manufacturing Anti-Semites

Nowadays this myth, too, is giving up its blessed soul. Whatever good the existence of the State of Israel may or may not have done, the current government of Israel is quickly undoing. [Prime Minister Ariel] Sharon's government is a giant laboratory for the growing of the anti-Semitism virus. It exports it to the whole world. Anti-Semitic organizations, which for many years vegetated on the margins of society, rejected and despised, are suddenly growing and flowering. Anti-Semitism, which had hidden itself in shame since World War II, is now riding on a great wave of opposition to Sharon's policy of oppression.

Sharon's propaganda agents are pouring oil on the flames by accusing all critics of his policy of being anti-Semites. Many good people, who feel no hatred at all towards the Jews but who detest the persecution of Palestinians, are now called anti-Semites. Thus the sting is taken out of this word, giving it something approaching respectability.

The practical upshot: not only is the State of Israel not protecting Jews from anti-Semitism, but—on the contrary—its government is manufacturing and exporting the anti-Semitism that threatens Jews around the world.

For many years, Israel enjoyed the sympathy of most people. It was seen as the state of Holocaust survivors, a small and courageous country defending itself against the repeated assaults of murderous Arabs. Slowly, this image has been replaced by another: a cruel, brutal, and colonizing state, oppressing a small and helpless people. The persecuted has become the persecutor: David has turned into Goliath.

> *Anti-Semitism, which had hidden itself in shame since World War II, is now riding on a great wave of opposition to [Prime Minister Ariel] Sharon's policy of oppression.*

We Israelis, living in a bubble of self-delusion, find it hard to imagine how the world sees us. In many countries, television and newspapers publish daily pictures of Palestinian children throwing stones at monstrous tanks, soldiers harassing women at checkpoints, despairing old men sitting on the ruins of their demolished homes, soldiers taking aim and shooting children. These soldiers do not look like human beings in uniform—the world does not see "the neighbor's son" most Israelis see. These soldiers look like robots without faces, armed to the teeth, heads hidden by helmets, bullet-proof vests changing their proportions. People who have seen these photos dozens and hundreds of times start to see the whole State of Israel in this image.

For Jews, this creates a dangerous, vicious circle. Sharon's actions create repulsion and opposition throughout the world. These actions reinforce anti-Semitism. Faced with this danger, Jewish organizations are pushed into defending Israel and giving it unqualified support. This support enables the anti-Semites to attack not only the government of Israel, or the State of Israel as a whole, but local Jews, too. And so on.

Anti-Semites of all stripes and hues are, of course, repulsive. They will vilify Jews whatever we do. Anti-Semitism, like other forms of racism, is never justified. But that is not the point. The point is that the actions of the Sharon government, and the unqualified support given to this government by the Jewish establishment, has enabled these hard-core anti-Semites to win over well-meaning people who are repelled by Sharon's actions.

Silencing Opposition to Sharon in the United States

The Israeli government pretends to speak for all Jews around the world, yet no attempt has been made by mainstream Jewish organizations to reject this claim. This may turn out to be a terrible mistake.

In Europe, Jews already feel the pressure to reject Sharon. But in the United States, Jews still feel supremely self-confident. In Europe, Jews have learned over the centuries that it is not wise to be too conspicuous and to display their wealth and influence. But in America, the very opposite is happening: the Jewish establishment is practically straining to prove that it controls the country.

Every few years, the Jewish lobby "eliminates" an American politician who does not support the Israeli government unconditionally. This is not done secretly, behind the scenes, but as a public "execution." [In November 2002] the Jewish establishment rallied against the black congresswoman Cynthia McKinney, a young, active, intelligent, and very sympathetic woman. She had dared to criticize the Sharon government, to support the Palestinian cause, and (worst of all from the Jewish establishment's standpoint) she had gained the support of Israeli and Jewish peace groups. The Jewish establishment found a counter-candidate, a practically unknown black woman, injected huge sums into the campaign, and defeated Cynthia.

> **❝** *[Jewish communities can] disarm anti-Semites by breaking the habit of automatically identifying with everything the Israeli government does.* **❞**

All this happened in the open, with fanfare, to make a public example of McKinney—so that every senator and congressperson would know that criticizing Sharon is tantamount to political suicide. Not content with this flexing of power, the pro-Israel lobby—which consists of Jews and extreme right-wing Christian fundamentalists—is now pushing the Bush administration to start a war in Iraq [U.S. invasion of Iraq began in March 2003]. This, too, openly and in full view of the American public. Dozens of articles in the important newspapers point out the Jewish pro-war influence as a plain political fact.

Of course, Jews have a right, just like every other citizen in the United States, to raise their voice in the political arena. But, as the ancients remind us, "pride comes before the fall." The shameless flaunting of Jewish power, the buying of representatives and senators, the immense pressure put on the media, is counterproductive in the long run. It is the ghetto mentality turned upside down; instead of timidity, arrogance.

What will happen if the war the pro-Israel lobby is advocating ends in failure? If it has unexpected negative results and many young Americans die? If the American public turns against it, as happened during the Vietnam War?

What will happen when Sharon's policies bring about revolution in the Arab world, as they will if he is allowed to continue on his current path? As long as the Jewish establishment can convince the American public that the interests of Israel and the United States are identical (an idiotic notion) this will not arouse anger, but when the day comes—and it will come—when the two countries' interests are seen as diverging, what will be the reaction then?

One can easily imagine a whispering campaign starting: "The Jews have pushed us into this." "The Jews support Israel more than they support America," and, finally, "The Jews control our country."

Of course, the special political culture of the United States encourages the rise of special interest groups—but that was also true in Spain of the Golden Age and in the Weimar Republic in Germany. History does not have to repeat itself, but neither should one disregard its lessons. Just because Jews can constitute a special interest group does not mean that creating a disproportionate influence over Congress and the White House is the best strategy for enhancing the future of the Jewish people.

"Seek Peace and Pursue It!"

There are people in Israel who secretly wish for the victory of anti-Semitism everywhere. That would confirm another Zionist myth on which we were brought up: that Jews will not be able to live anywhere but in Israel, because anti-Semitism is bound to triumph everywhere. But the United States is not France or Argentina; it plays a critical role in the Middle East. Israel's national security, as established by all Israeli governments since Ben-Gurion [Israel's first prime minister], is based on total support from the United States—military, political, and economic.

If I were asked for advice, I would counsel Jewish communities throughout the world as follows: break out of the vicious circle. Disarm anti-Semites by breaking the habit of automatically identifying with everything the Israeli government does. Let your conscience speak out. Return to the traditional Jewish values of "That which is altogether just shalt thou follow!" (Deut. 16:20) and "Seek peace and pursue it!" (Psal. 4: 14). Identify yourselves with the Other Israel, which is struggling to uphold these values at home.

All over the world, new Jewish groups that follow this way are multiplying. They break yet another myth, that the duty of Jews everywhere is to subordinate themselves to the edicts of the current Israeli government. They know that the true duty of Jews worldwide is to cling fast to Jewish values.

5

Criticizing Israeli Policies Concerning Palestinians Is Not Anti-Semitic

Nada Elia

Dr. Nada Elia, a writer and teacher who now lives in the United States, was born in Palestine to parents who became refugees in 1948 and then fled to Lebanon. She is the author and editor of over twenty-five articles, including "Epistemic Violence, Smear Campaigns, and Hit-Lists: Disappearing the Palestinians."

Long before the Palestinians began using terrorism and suicide bombings, Israel pursued a policy of violently dispossessing Palestinians. Israel has used terror, assassination, intimidation, and land confiscation to drive Palestinians from their land. In 1948 Israeli gunmen forced many Palestinians from their houses and villages. The Palestinians call this dispossession "Al Nakba" or "The Catastrophe." Israel has long denied this policy of dispossession and refuses to recognize the rights of the indigenous population of Palestinians who have been displaced. When Palestinians try to talk about their dispossession and their rights, Israelis accuse them of being anti-Semitic in an effort to silence them and cover up the truth of what actually happened to the Palestinians. However, if the wrongs done to the Palestinians were openly acknowledged and their rights recognized, the suicide bombings could stop, and Israel and Palestine could move toward justice and peace.

Having been called anti-Semitic practically every time I have criticized Zionism, I have learned not to let myself be gagged by the charge, and remain fully convinced that a critique of a political ideology cannot correctly be equated with racist hostility towards an entire ethnic group, which includes among its members some—even a majority—of people who hold the political belief I oppose. Nor will my silence protect me, so I continue to express myself, even if my views are considered problematic. So let me speak. Let me tell you about Al Nakba [1948 Palestinian dispossession] and the first terrorist attacks in Palestine.

> // When Israel took over almost 80 percent of Palestine in 1948, it did so through settlement and ethnic cleansing of the original Palestinian population. //

It is easy to present the recent Israeli attacks on Palestinian refugee camps as retaliation against the suicide bombings carried on by "Palestinian terrorists" against "innocent Israeli civilians." But Israel had aggressively pursued an armed policy of dispossession since before its creation in 1948, long before there was a single Palestinian terrorist, as evident from the following choice statements made by Israeli leaders over the last 54 years. I will restrict myself to a few examples, although they can unfortunately fill volumes.

Dispossessing the Palestinians

Addressing his General Staff in 1948, David Ben-Gurion [Israel's first prime minister] explained his plan for the region: "We should prepared to go on the offensive. Our aim is to smash Lebanon, Trans-Jordan, and Syria. The weak point is Lebanon, for the Muslim regime is artificial and easy to undermine. We shall establish a Christian state there, and then we shall smash the Arab legion, eliminate Trans-Jordan. Syria will fall to us. We then bomb and move on to take Port Said, Alexandria, and Sinai." There were no suicide bombers against Israeli civilians in 1948, as Ben-Gurion aimed to smash Lebanon, Trans-Jordan, and Syria, and seize parts of Egypt.

Nor were there any Palestinian suicide bombers against innocent Israeli civilians in 1967, when Israel occupied more Palestinian land; simply the belief, articulated by [the head of the Jewish Agency's Colonization Department in 1940] Joseph Weitz in *Diaries and Letters to the Children*, that "It should be clear that there is no room for both peoples to live in this country. . . . Not one village, not one tribe must remain. They must be moved to Iraq, Syria, or even Trans-Jordan." "Not one tribe must remain" certainly sounds like ethnic cleansing, and so does "rid[ding] the Galilee of its Arab population," which Israel Koenig, then Northern District commissioner, wrote in a secret report to then Prime Minister Yitzhak Rabin, and where he explains: "We must use terror, assassination, intimidation, land confiscation, and the cutting of all social services to rid the Galilee of its Arab population." Ethnic cleansing, terror, and assassination were Zionist policy long before the first Palestinian suicide bomber first saw the light of day, under occupation, as a refugee in his own land.

Anti-Palestinian Racism

Nor were there any Palestinian suicide bombers in 1982, when, having driven millions of Palestinians into neighboring countries, Israel invaded Lebanon in order to kill thousands more, then living in the utmost squalor in camps outside of Beirut. There were no suicide bombers in 1982, when [Prime Minister] Menachem Begin, in a speech to the Israeli Knesset during the invasion, claimed the Palestinians "are two-legged beasts." There were no suicide bombers when Rafael Eitan, chief of staff of the Israeli "Defense" Forces, explained a few months later: "We shall use the ultimate force until the Palestinians come crawling to us on all fours."

These statements, all made before the first Palestinian suicide bombing against innocent Israeli civilians, reveal the virulent racism of the Zionist founders and leaders of the Jewish state. Thus when Interior Minister Uzi Landau claims, in April of 2002, that "we are not facing human beings, but rather beasts," he is not driven to such a statement by the ferocity of the latest suicide bombing against innocent Israeli civilians in Israel. Rather, he continues in a long line of Israeli politicians who have made similar statements since the creation of Israel.

Yet I am called anti-Semitic if I criticize Zionism, the movement that called for, and actively continues to implement, the ethnic cleansing of one people in order to allow for the creation of a "Jewish" state. The Jewish National Land Fund laws keep land ownership for the exclusive use of Jews. That, I am told, is not racist. But anyone who criticizes Israel as an exclusionary apartheid state is racist, or guilty of hijacking "important issues," because a discussion of the victimization of Palestinians is always besides the point, must always be subordinate to other issues. Can my feminist friends tell me why anti-Semitism is a prominent feminist issue, but a discussion of anti-Palestinian racism is not, as [feminist] Betty Friedan, tried to explain to Egyptian feminist Nawal Saadawi at the United Nations International Conference on women in Nairobi, [Kenya,] urging her: "Please do not bring up Palestine in your speech. This is a women's conference, not a political conference."

Israel's Denial of Dispossession

You didn't know the first terrorists in the Middle East were the Zionists. I believe you. Israel has long denied its responsibility for the violent theft of land that occurred in 1948, as Palestinians were forced from their villages at the point of Israeli guns. We Palestinians refer to that armed dispossession as *Al Nakba*, meaning "The Catastrophe." Israel continues to silence it. As a doctoral student at Oxford University, Ilan Pappe chose 1948 as the subject of his dissertation, finding strong evidence of the forceful removal of the Palestinians from their homes. He writes: "When Israel took over almost 80 percent of Palestine in 1948, it did so through settlement and ethnic cleansing of the original Palestinian population," adding "Needless to say, what I found also contradicted the messages conveyed to me as a citizen of Israel during my initiation in the army, at public events such as Independence Day, and in daily discourse in the country's media on the history of the Israeli-Palestinian conflict."

That daily discourse dates back to the early days of Zionism, with such illustrious thinkers as Israel Zangwill writing in 1901 that "Palestine is a land without people for people without a land." Zangwill had not been to the Middle East and, to his credit, he retracted his statement in 1920. But Golda Meir, the former Israeli Prime Minister much admired by my antiracist feminist friends, simply declared in 1969 that Palestinians didn't exist. "There was no such thing as a Palestinian people in Palestine," she explained to the *London Sunday Times*. "It was as though there was a Palestinian people and we came and threw them out and took their country from them. They did not exist."

If there were no people in Palestine in 1948 (only beasts?), then nobody was hurt by the creation of Israel. The Nakba never happened. This censorship of the events of 1948 continues to this day: the Israeli Knesset has passed as law preventing any Israeli negotiator from even discussing the Right of Return of the Palestinian refugees to the homes they had occupied before 1948, and then–Prime Minister Ehud Barak made a public commitment to it on the stairs of the plane flying him to Camp David. More recently, in November 2001, an M.A. [master's] student was expelled from Haifa University in Israel for exposing a hitherto-unknown Israeli massacre carried out against the Palestinians in 1948. In May 2002, Pappe himself [faced] expulsion from that university, where he [was] a professor of political science, as a result of his support of this student and of academic freedom generally.

> **❝** Will my anti-racist friends finally recognize the tortured humanity of the millions of Palestinians, who have been terrorized, displaced, dispossessed [and] humiliated . . . by Zionism since 1948? **❞**

If the wrongs against innocent Palestinian civilians will not even be acknowledged, how can they be redressed? Will my anti-racist friends finally recognize the tortured humanity of the millions of Palestinians, who have been terrorized, displaced, dispossessed, humiliated and otherwise wronged by Zionism since 1948, and who are now so conveniently overshadowed by the suicide bombers? Will any political leaders and grassroots activists seriously work on redressing those wrongs? A very likely consequence of such a just, ethical, moral, anti-racist endeavor would be the end of suicide bombings against innocent Israeli civilians, as justice gives way to peace. Imagine peace in the Middle East. . . . The Arabic word for peace is Salaam, and still-hopeful Palestinian parents name their children Salaam, and Huriya (freedom), and Nihaya ("the end"). Imagine the end of diaspora, exile, misery, suffering. The end of refugee camps. . . .

I have just finished reading [novelist] Carol Shields' *The Stone Diaries*. In the opening pages is this description of a door-to-door peddler in early twentieth-century Canada:

"It's hard nowadays to talk about the old Jew. It's a tricky business. The brain's got to be folded all the way back to the time when the words 'old Jew' could be said straight out: old Jew; here comes the old Jew."

> **"***Imagine the day I will no longer be called anti-Semitic simply because I denounce the racism of my oppressor.***"**

A pang of pain shot through me as I read that reflection. For I yearn with all my being for the day when a novel will be written speaking of the days, long ago, when it was considered acceptable to dehumanize Palestinians. A novel recalling that sad episode in Israeli history, the denial of the racist ethnic cleansing of the Palestinians.

But I am writing this in the early twenty-first century, and it looks like it may be another century before such an opening could be written about Palestinians. Imagine:

"It's hard nowadays to talk about the Arab terrorist. It's a tricky business. The brain's got to be folded all the way back to the time when the words 'Arab terrorist' could be said straight out: Arab terrorist; here comes the Arab terrorist."

Imagine the day Arabs who believe in freedom, justice, dignity, and human rights for all are no longer considered terrorists. Imagine the day I will no longer be called anti-Semitic simply because I denounce the racism of my oppressor, the day I will no longer be called fanatic simply because I want an end to the occupation of my homeland. My mother is from Maskabiya, my father from Misrara, but I have never seen Palestine. All I have ever known is the Diaspora, and the racism of people who are disturbed by my mere existence, and persistence. My two-legged humanity. Imagine my being granted the right of return.

I can only dream on, though. It is no longer possible to deny the Nakba, thanks to the concerted effort of a minority of Palestinians within Israel since 1988, the fortieth anniversary of the catastrophic loss of land and rights. But the public mood in Israel today seems to call for more of the same. Should [Israeli prime minister] Ariel Sharon wish to repeat the ethnic cleansing of the Palestinians in the territories occupied since 1967, he has the support of the majority of his people. "Let him finish the job" is heard at an alarming rate both in Israel and the U.S. Crimes against humanity will continue to be overlooked when perpetrated by Israel. [Former U.S. secretary of state] Colin Powell "did not see any evidence of a massacre in Jenin [a Palestinian town]." Colin Powell did not think it important to look. And should Sharon wish to "transfer" non-Jewish citizens of Israel to various countries willing to accept them, he has the support of the majority of his people.

And should I criticize Israeli policy, the policy which allowed for the creation and defense of a "Jewish state" founded on the ethnic cleansing of all non-Jews, my anti-racist "friends" call me anti-Semitic.

6

Denying Jews the Right to a Homeland Is Anti-Semitic

Michael Melchior

Michael Melchior, a member of the Israeli Knesset, or parliament, since 1999, is a former deputy minister of foreign affairs. He is also the international director of the Elie Wiesel Foundation for Humanity, which promotes human rights.

In the twentieth century, anti-Semitism led to the ultimate crime—the Holocaust, the systematic attempt to exterminate the Jews. Shortly after the Holocaust occurred, the Jewish state of Israel was founded. The establishment of Israel as a secure homeland for all Jews was the fulfillment of a dream of the Zionists, or Jewish nationalists. Despite Israel's recognition of equal rights for all its inhabitants, it is often accused of being racist, and its very existence is constantly under attack by its Arab neighbors. Denying Israel's right to exist is anti-Zionist and anti-Semitic. Anti-Zionist statements made by the Palestinians and other nationalities are anti-Semitic and only serve to increase racism in the world and decrease the chance for peace in the Middle East.

W hy, when the world was created, did God create just one man, Adam, and one woman, Eve? The Rabbis answered: so that all humankind would come from a single union, to teach us that we are all brothers and sisters.

This Conference [against Racism] was dedicated to that

Michael Melchior, statement to the World Conference Against Racism, Durban, South Africa, September 3, 2001.

simple proposition. We, all of us, have a common lineage, and are all, irrespective of race, religion or gender, created in the divine image. Indeed, this single idea, unknown to all other ancient civilizations, may be the greatest gift that the Jewish people has given to the world, the recognition of the equality and dignity of every human being.

The foremost right that follows from this principle is the right to be free, not to be a slave. It is imperative that the international community address and duly acknowledge, already far far too late, the magnitude of the tragedy of slavery.

The horror of slavery is profoundly engraved in the experience of the Jewish people—a people formed in slavery. For hundreds of years the children of Israel were enslaved in Egypt until, as the Book of Exodus recounts, the call: 'Let my people go' heralded the first national liberation movement in history, and the model for every liberation which was to follow.

The Jewish response to slavery was remarkable. Rather than forget or sublimate the suffering of slavery, Jewish tradition insisted that every Jew must remember and relive it. And to this day, on Passover, every Jewish family reenacts the experience of slavery, eats the bread of affliction, and appreciates once again the taste of freedom. Through the ages of our exile this psychodrama has had a profound impact on the Jewish psyche: making sure that every child born into comfort knows the pains of oppression, and every child born into oppression knows the hope of redemption.

But remembrance of our suffering as slaves has a more important function—to remind ourselves of our moral obligations. The experience of oppression brings no privilege, but rather responsibility. We have a responsibility to protect the weak, the widow and the orphan and the stranger, because as the Bible says: "You yourselves were strangers in the land of Egypt." Even God, in the first and most fundamental of the 10 commandments, identifies Himself not as 'Creator of the World' or 'Splitter of the Red Sea', but as 'the One who freed you from slavery'.

And indeed in every country in which they have lived, Jews have been in the forefront of the battle for human rights and freedom from oppression. The same urge for national liberation, that led to the Exodus, and that led to the Zionist dream that Jews could live in freedom in their land, was intrinsically bound up with the belief that not just one people, but all peoples must be free. It was this conviction that Theodor Herzl, the founder of the Zionist movement [to found the state of Israel] expressed in his book *Altneuland*, as early as 1902:

"There is still one problem of racial misfortune unsolved. The depths of that problem only a Jew can comprehend. I refer to the problem of the Blacks. Just call to mind all those terrible episodes of the slave trade, of human beings who merely because they were black were stolen like cattle, taken prisoners, captured and sold. Their children grew up in strange lands, the objects of contempt and hostility because their complexions were different. I am not ashamed to say, though I may expose myself to ridicule for saying so, that once I have witnessed the redemption of Israel, my people, I wish to assist the redemption of the Black people."

As Herzl understood, remembrance of slavery is integral to the Jewish experience. A Jew cannot be truly free if he or she does not have compassion on those who are enslaved.

The Ultimate Hatred

If slavery is one form of racist atrocity, antisemitism is another. And by antisemitism, let us be clear, we mean the hatred of Jews. The word 'antisemitism' was deliberately coined in 1879 by Wilhelm Marr, an anti-Jewish racist in Germany, to replace the term judenhass, Jew-hatred, which had gone out of favor. It has always, and only, been used to describe hatred and discrimination directed at Jews. Attempts to eradicate the plain meaning of the word are not only anti-semitic, indeed they are anti-semantic.

Those uncomfortable recognizing the existence of antisemitism not only try to redefine the term, they try to deny that it is different from any other form of discrimination. But it is a unique form of hatred. It is directed at those of particular birth, irrespective of their faith, and those of particular faith, irrespective of their birth. It is the oldest and most persistent form of group hatred; in our century this ultimate hatred has led to the ultimate crime, the Holocaust.

But antisemitism goes far beyond hatred of Jews. It has arisen where Jews have never lived, and survives where only Jewish cemeteries remain. And while Jews may be the first to suffer from its influence, they have rarely been the last.

Antisemitism reveals the inner corruption of a society, because at its root it is fueled by a rejection of the humane and moral values the Jewish people bequeathed to the world. As

Anne Frank, the Jewish schoolgirl in hiding from the Nazis in occupied Amsterdam, wrote in her Diary:

"If we bear all this suffering and if there are still Jews left, when it is over, then Jews, instead of being doomed, will be held up as an example. Who knows, it might even be our religion from which the world and all peoples learn good, and for that reason only do we now suffer."

Anne Frank was murdered by the Nazis in Bergen-Belsen [concentration camp] for being a Jew, just one of over one million Jewish children to be killed in the Holocaust.

Those who cannot bring themselves to recognize the unique evil of antisemitism, similarly cannot accept the stark fact of the Holocaust, the first systematic attempt to destroy an entire people. The past decade has witnessed an alarming increase in attempts to deny the simple fact of this atrocity, at the very time that the Holocaust is passing from living memory to history. After wiping out 6 million Jewish lives, there are those who would wipe out their deaths. At this Conference, too, we have witnessed a vile attempt to generalize and pluralize the word 'Holocaust', and to empty it of its meaning as a reference to a specific historic event with a clear and vital message for all humanity.

Could there be anything worse than to brutally, systematically annihilate a people; to take the proud Jews of [the cities of] Vilna, Warsaw, Minsk, Lodz; to burn their holy books, to steal their dignity, their freedom, their hair, their teeth, to turn them into numbers, to slaves, to the ashes of Auschwitz, Treblinka, Majdanek and Dachau [concentration camps]? Could anything be worse that this? And the answer is yes, there is something even worse: to do such a thing, and then to deny it, to trivialize it, to take from the mourners, the children and the grandchildren, the legitimacy of their grief, and from all humanity the urgent lesson that might stop it happening again. . . .

The Establishment of Israel

The 20th century which witnessed the atrocities of the Holocaust also witnessed the fulfillment of the Zionist dream, the reestablishment of a Jewish state in Israel's historic land. For Zionism is quite simply that—the national movement of the Jewish people, based on an unbroken connection, going back some 4000 years, between the People of the Book and the Land of the Bible. It is like the liberation movements of Africa and Asia, the national liberation movement of the Jewish people.

And it is a movement of which other national liberation movements can be justly proud. It has strived continually to establish a society which reflects the highest ideals of democracy and justice for all its inhabitants, in which Jew and Arab can live together, in which women and men have equal rights, in which there is freedom of thought and of expression, and in which all have access to the judicial process to ensure these rights are protected.

The aspiration to build such a society was enshrined from the outset in Israel's Declaration of Independence:

"The State of Israel . . . will foster the development of the country for the benefit of all its inhabitants; it will ensure complete equality of social and political rights to all its inhabitants, irrespective of creed, race or gender; it will guarantee freedom of religion, conscience, language, education and culture."

It is a tall task. It is a constant struggle. And we do not always succeed. But, even in the face of the open hostility of its neighbors and continued threats to its existence, there are few countries that have made such efforts to realize such a vision. Few countries of Israel's age and size have welcomed immigrants from over one hundred countries, of all colors and tongues, sent medical aid and disaster relief to alleviate human tragedy wherever it strikes, maintained a free press, including the freest Arabic press anywhere in the Middle East.

Anti-Zionism Is Antisemitic

And yet those who cannot bring themselves to say the words 'the Holocaust', or to recognize antisemitism for the evil that it is, would have us condemn the 'racist practices of Zionism'. Did any one of those Arab states which conceived this obscenity stop for one moment to consider their own record? Or to think, for that matter, of the situation of the Jews and other minorities in their own countries?

These states would have us believe that they are anti-Zionist, not antisemitic, but again and again this lie is disproved. What are the despicable caricatures of Jews that fill the Arab press and are being circulated at this Conference: what are the vicious libels so freely invented and disseminated by our enemies— about the use of poison gas, or depleted uranium bullets, or injecting babies with the AIDS virus—if not the reincarnation of age-old antisemitic canards?

To criticize policies of the Government of Israel—or of any

country—is legitimate, even vital; indeed as a democratic state many Israelis do just that. But there is profound difference between criticizing a country, and denying its right to exist. Anti-Zionism, the denial of Jews the basic right to a home, is nothing but antisemitism, pure and simple. As Dr. Martin Luther King Jr. wrote:

"You declare, my friend, that you do not hate the Jews, you are merely 'anti-Zionist'. And I say, let the truth ring forth from the high mountain tops. Let it echo through the valleys of God's green earth: When people criticize Zionism they mean Jews. . . . Zionism is nothing less than the dream and ideal of the Jewish people returning to live in their own land. . . . And what is anti-Zionism? It is the denial to the Jew of the fundamental right that we justly claim for the people of Africa and freely accord to all other nations of the globe. It is discrimination against Jews because they are Jews. In short it is antisemitism."

> *Antisemitism reveals the inner corruption of a society, because at its root it is fueled by a rejection of the humane and moral values the Jewish people bequeathed to the world.*

The venal hatred of Jews that has taken the form of anti-Zionism, and which has surfaced at this Conference is, however, different in one crucial way from the antisemitism of the past. Today it is being deliberately propagated and manipulated for political ends. Children are not born as racists, racism is a result of lack of education and political manipulation. And today generations of Palestinian children are being deliberately and systematically indoctrinated, with textbooks stained with blood libels [antisemitic propaganda] and children's television programs dripping with hatred. This high risk strategy is bound to fail, but it will exact a heavy price.

The conflict between us and our Palestinian neighbors is not racial, and has no place at this Conference. It is political and territorial, and as such can and should be resolved to end the suffering and bring peace and security to the Israeli and Palestinian peoples. The path towards such a resolution is clear: an immediate cessation of violence and terror and a return to negotiations as recommended by the Mitchell Committee Report which both parties have accepted. The outrageous and manic accusations we have heard here are attempts to turn a political issue into a racial one, with almost no hope of resolution.

[Between July 11–24, 2000] at Camp David, the Israeli Government demonstrated its deep commitment to peace by offering our Palestinian neighbors far-reaching compromises. These compromises, you will recall, were applauded by the entire international community. But, the Palestinians did not accept these proposals, nor did they put forward any compromise proposals of their own. To our deep dismay they responded with a wave of violence. Over the past year [2001] this violence has escalated into protracted and inhuman attacks on the Israeli civilian population, forcing Israel to assume a role we abhor, defending our citizens by military means which we had hoped and prayed would be relegated to the past.

I will not refer here to the disappointing statement we have heard from the head of the Palestinian Authority. Rather than utilize this vital forum to inspire his own people, and the people of the world, to seek peace, honor and harmony, he chose to use this podium to incite to bitterness and hatred. Another missed opportunity by the leader of the Palestinian people.

My own cousins, two little daughters and their brother, lost their legs only a few weeks ago in a terrorist attack on a bus carrying children to school. Many Palestinian children have likewise been wounded for life. The vicious libels, the delegitimization and dehumanization we have heard at this Conference will do nothing to prevent more Israeli and Palestinian mothers and fathers bringing their young ones to their graves.

> *Anti-Zionism, the denial of Jews the basic right to a home, is nothing but antisemitism, pure and simple.*

But here today, something greater even than peace in the Middle East is being sacrificed—the highest values of humanity. Racism, in all its forms, is one of the most widespread and pernicious evils, depriving millions of hope and fundamental rights. It might have been hoped that this first Conference of the 21st century would have taken up the challenge of, if not eradicating racism, at least disarming it: But instead humanity is being sacrificed to a political agenda. Barely a decade after the UN repealed the infamous 'Zionism is Racism' resolution [1975] which Secretary-General Kofi Annan described, with characteristic understatement, as a "low point" in the history of the United Nations, a group of states for whom the terms 'racism', 'discrimination', and even 'human rights' simply do not appear in their domestic lexicon, have hijacked this Conference and plunged us to even greater depths.

Can there be a greater irony than the fact that a conference convened to combat the scourge of racism should give rise to the most racist declaration in a major international organization since the Second World War?

Despite the vicious antisemitism we have heard here, I do not fear for the Jewish people, which has learned to be resilient and to hold fast to its faith.

Despite the virulent incitement against my country, I do not fear for Israel, which has the strength not just of courage, but also of conviction.

But I do fear, deeply, for the victims of racism. For the slaves, the disenfranchised, the oppressed, the inexplicably hated, the impoverished, the despised, the millions who turn their eyes to this hall, in the frail hope that it may address their suffering. Who see instead that a blind and venal hatred of the Jews has turned their hopes into a farce. For them I fear.

We are here as representatives of states, and states of their nature have political interests and agendas. But we are also human beings, all of us brothers and sisters created in the divine image. And in those quiet moments when we recognize our common humanity, and look into our soul, let us consider what we came here to do—and what we have in fact done:

We came to learn from our history, but we find it being buried to hide its lessons.

We came to communicate in the language of humanity, but we hear its vocabulary twisted beyond all comprehension.

We came out of respect for the sacred values entrusted to us, but see them here perverted for political ends.

And ultimately, we came to serve the victims of racism, but have witnessed yet another atrocity, committed in their name.

7

Criticizing the Israeli Government Is Not Anti-Semitic

Allan C. Brownfeld

Syndicated columnist Allan C. Brownfeld, who specializes in writing about the peoples and issues of the Middle East, is also the editor of Issues, *a journal published by the American Council for Judaism, an organization dedicated to the advancement of Judaism as a religion of universal ideals and human values.*

Many Jews living both inside and outside Israel regularly criticize Israel's government. This criticism is a healthy part of a democratic society. However, some supporters of Israel argue that to criticize Israel's policies is anti-Semitic. This view strangles discussion of issues such as Israel's treatment of the Palestinians and the legality of the Israeli settlements in the Palestinian territories of the West Bank and Gaza. Because no one wants to be called anti-Semitic, the label can be used to intimidate Palestinians and silence debate over Israel's Middle East policy. Redefining anti-Semitism as opposition to or criticism of Israel not only threatens free speech, but it also trivializes the real meaning of anti-Semitism. This new definition of anti-Semitism excludes and marginalizes the numerous American and Israeli Jews who speak out against Israel's policies. Achieving peace in the Middle East requires honest and open discussion. It is therefore harmful to suppress such debate through the misuse of the term *anti-Semitism*.

Allan C. Brownfeld, "Is It Anti-Semitic to Criticize Israel and Its Policies?" *Washington Report on Middle East Affairs*, vol. 21, June/July 2002, p. 69. Copyright © 2002 by American Educational Trust. All rights reserved. Reproduced by permission.

As developments in the Middle East—from Palestinian suicide bombers to Israeli incursions into Palestinian territory to the assault upon [the Palestinian town of] Jenin—continue to be the focus of attention both in the U.S. and throughout the world, we have seen a growing campaign to silence any criticism of Israel and its policies as being, somehow, "anti-Semitic."

Sadly, genuine anti-Semitism has been seen in parts of Europe with the burning of synagogues, the desecration of cemeteries and assaults upon individuals. It is in the United States, however, that the charge is made that criticism of Israel represents a new kind of anti-Semitism. The Anti-Defamation League [an organization that fights religious and racial discrimination] declares that, "Anti-Zionism is showing its true colors as deep-rooted anti-Semitism." In an article, "The Return of Anti-Semitism," published in the February 2002 issue of *Commentary*, Hillel Halkin, one of the magazine's regular contributors, states that ". . . one cannot be against Israel or Zionism, as opposed to this or that Israeli policy or Zionist position, without being anti-Semitic. Israel is the state of the Jews. Zionism is the belief that Jews should have a state. To defame Israel is to defame the Jews. . . ."

Halkin notes that, "Only an anti-Semite can systematically accuse Israel of what they are not guilty of." He proceeds to declare that, "Even this is not putting it strongly enough. There are times when only an anti-Semite can accuse Israel of what it is guilty of. . . . We must not give an inch on this point. The new anti-Israelism is nothing but the old anti-Semitism in disguise."

Rabbi Michael Melchior, Israel's deputy foreign minister, states that, "The anti-Semites during the ages had excuses, they've had different disguises. The new anti-Semitism has its centrality in the attacks against the existence of the Jewish state."

The tendency to label the criticism of Israel as anti-Semitism is hardly new, and has been an effective way to stifle free and open debate.

Accusations of Anti-Semitism

In a September 1983 *Commentary* article entitled "J'Accuse," Norman Podhoretz charged America's leading journalists, newspapers and television networks with "anti-Semitism" because of their reporting on the war in Lebanon and their criticism of Israel's conduct. Among those so accused were Anthony Lewis of *The New York Times*, Nicholas von Hoffman,

Joseph Harsch of *The Christian Science Monitor*, Rowland Evans, Robert Novak, Mary McGrory, Richard Cohen and Alfred Friendly of *The Washington Post*, and a host of others. These individuals and their news organizations were not criticized for poor reporting or lax journalistic standards; instead they were the subject of the charge of anti-Semitism.

"The war in Lebanon," Podhoretz wrote, "triggered an explosion of invective against Israel that in its fury and its reach was unprecedented in the public discourse in this country. In the past, unambiguously venomous attacks on Israel had been confined to marginal sectors of American political culture . . . the beginning of wisdom in thinking about this issue is to recognize that the vilification of Israel is the phenomenon to be addressed, not the Israeli behavior that supposedly provoked it. . . . What am I or anyone else going to say of those for whom there is nothing obvious about the assertion that in this particular case the reaction was disproportionate? From such people one is tempted to turn away in disgust. . . . We are dealing here with an eruption of anti-Semitism."

But the U.S. news media were hardly more critical of the Israeli role in Lebanon than the media in Israel. Moreover, while Podhoretz eagerly endorsed every twist and turn of [Israeli prime minister] Menachem Begin's policy in Lebanon, Israelis themselves became increasingly disenchanted.

To understand Podhoretz, Halkin and their colleagues, we must recognize that the term "anti-Semitic" is undergoing a major transformation. Until recently, those guilty of this offense were widely understood to be those who irrationally disliked Jews and Judaism. Now, however, the term is used in a far different way—one which threatens not only free speech but also threatens to trivialize anti-Semitism itself.

Anti-Semitism has been redefined as anything that opposes the policies and interests of Israel. The beginning of this redefinition may be said to date, in part, from the 1974 publication of the book *The New Anti-Semitism* by Arnold Forster and Benjamin R. Epstein, leaders of the Anti-Defamation League of B'nai B'rith.

Anti-Semitism Redefined

The nature of the "new" anti-Semitism, according to Forster and Epstein, is not necessarily hostility toward Jews as Jews, or toward Judaism, but, instead, a critical attitude of Israel and its policies. To such "anti-Semites," they wrote, "Jews are tolerable, acceptable in their particularity, only as victims, and when their situation changes so that they are either no longer victims or appear not to be, the non-Jewish world finds this so hard to take that the effort is begun to render them victims anew. . . . Many of the anti-Israel statements from non-Jewish sources, often the most respectable, carry an undeniable anti-Jewish message."

In the 1980s, Nathan Perlmutter, then director of the Anti-Defamation League, set forth the thesis that, "There has been a transformation of American anti-Semitism in recent times. The crude anti-Jewish bigotry once so commonplace . . . is today gauche. . . . Poll after poll indicates that Jews are one of America's highly regarded groups."

> *It is . . . easier to silence criticism with charges of anti-Semitism than to confront the complex realities of the Middle East.*

While what everyone understood to be anti-Semitism had been largely excised from American society, except on its extremist fringe, Perlmutter refused to declare victory over such bigotry. Instead, he redefined it. "The search for peace in the Middle East is littered with mine fields for Jewish interests," he declared. "Jewish concerns are confronted by the Semitically neutral postures of those who believe that if only Israel would yield this or that, the Middle East would become tranquil and the West's highway to its strategic interests and profits in the Persian Gulf would be secure. But at what cost to Israel's security? Israel's security, plainly said, means more to Jews today than their standing in the opinion polls."

Perlmutter substituted the term "Jewish interests" for what are, in reality, "Israeli interests." By changing the terms of the debate, he helped to create a situation in which anyone who is critical of Israel becomes, ipso facto, "anti-Semitic."

Former Under Secretary of State George Ball, a frequent critic of U.S. Middle East policy, was described in a public letter by Morris Abram, former president of the American Jewish Committee, as "one who is willing to accept and spread age-old calumnies about Jews." It was Ball's view that silence has been imposed upon the discussion of Middle East policy by the broad use of the charge of anti-Semitism: "Most people are terribly concerned not to be accused of being anti-Semitic," he noted, "and the lobby so often equates criticism of Israel with anti-Semitism. They keep pounding away at the theme, and people are deterred from speaking out."

The tactic of using the term "anti-Semitism" as a weapon against dissenters from Israeli policy is not really new. Dorothy Thompson, the distinguished journalist who was one of the earliest enemies of Nazism, found herself criticizing the policies of Israel shortly after its creation. Despite her valiant crusade against Hitler she, too, was subject to the charge of anti-Semitism. In an April 6, 1951, letter to *The Jewish Newsletter*, she wrote: "Really, I think continued emphasis should be put upon the extreme danger to the Jewish community of branding people like myself anti-Semitic. . . . The State of Israel has got to learn to live in the same atmosphere of free criticism which every other state in the world must endure. . . . There are many subjects on which writers in this country are, because of these pressures, becoming craven and mealy-mouthed. But people don't like to be craven and mealy-mouthed; every time one yields to such pressure, one is filled with self-contempt and this self-contempt works itself out in resentment of those who caused it."

A quarter-century later, in the Feb. 5, 1975, edition of the *Washington Star*, columnist Carl Rowan reported that, "When I wrote my recent column about what I perceive to be a subtle erosion of support for Israel in this town, I was under no illusion as to what the reaction would be. I was prepared for a barrage of letters to me and newspapers carrying my column and accusing me of being 'anti-Semitic.'. . . The mail rolling in has met my worst expectations. . . . This whining, baseless name-calling is a certain way to turn friends into enemies."

The notion that criticism of Israel is "anti-Semitic" fails to confront the large number of Jews, both Americans and Israelis, who are in the forefront of criticizing Israeli policies, often charging that such policies violate traditional Jewish values.

In April [2002], the Israeli human rights group B'Tselem charged that Israel has tortured Palestinians who have been detained for interrogation during its April military offensive. The group said that the interrogation methods included breaking the toes of prisoners. The detainees also have been prohibited from meeting with lawyers, the group said. Is B'Tselem anti-Semitic?

Writing in the April 25 [2002] issue of *The New York Times Review of Books*, Anthony Lewis stated that, in the end, "There can be peace only when Israel withdraws from the territories it conquered in 1967, leaving an uninterrupted West Bank as part of a viable Palestinian state. . . . A solution along the lines of [Saudi Arabian] Crown Prince Abdullah's proposal would entail risks for Israel, of course. Suicide attacks might still continue. But such a solution is a better gamble than a policy that has aroused antagonism toward Israel in much of the world. Zionism, with its noble goal of a Jewish national homeland, faces the ultimate test of its legitimacy, whether it will accept limits, accept that another people has a legitimate claim to a national home in Palestine." Is Anthony Lewis anti-Semitic?

Israel as Pariah

In England, Gerald Kaufman, a prominent figure in Britain's Jewish community and a member of Parliament, said that [Israeli prime minister] Ariel Sharon's policies "are staining the Star of David [a symbol of Judaism] with blood." He described Sharon as a "blustering bully" and declared: "It's time to remind Sharon that the Star of David belongs to all Jews and not to his repulsive government. Now, the state of Israel is a ghetto, an international pariah." Is Gerald Kaufman anti-Semitic?

Needless to say, we could fill many pages with Jewish criticism of Israel. Responding to the notion that critics of Israel are anti-Semitic, *Washington Post* columnist Richard Cohen writes on April 30, 2002, that, "If I weren't a Jew, I might be called an anti-Semite. I have occasionally been critical of Israel. I have occasionally taken the Palestinians' side. I have always maintained that the occupation of the West Bank is wrong and while I am, to my marrow, a supporter of Israel, I insist that the Palestinian cause—although sullied by terrorism—is a worthy one. In Israel itself, these positions would hardly be considered remarkable. People with similar views serve in parliament. They write columns for the newspapers. . . . I cannot say the same about America. Here, criticism of Israel, particularly anti-Zionism, is equated with anti-Semitism."

Cohen said that, "To turn a deaf ear to the demands of Palestinians, to dehumanize them all as bigots only exacerbates hatred on both sides. The Palestinians do have a case. Their methods are sometimes—maybe often—execrable, but that does not change the fact that they are a people without a state. As long as that persists so too will their struggle. . . . To protest living conditions on the West Bank is not anti-Semitic. To condemn the increasing encroachment of Jewish settlements is not anti-Semitic. . . . To suggest, finally, that Ariel Sharon is a rejectionist who provocatively egged on the Palestinians is not anti-Semitism. . . ."

Many in Israel are also critical of labeling criticism of their government's policies as "anti-Semitism." Professor David Newman, chairman of the department of politics and government at Ben-Gurion University of the Negev and editor of the *International Journal of Geopolitics,* states that, "A country that continually uses, and all too often manipulates, Holocaust imagery to justify its policies of self-defense and 'never again,' cannot complain when the rest of the world uses those same standards to make judgments concerning its own policies. We used to play a game of make-believe and convince ourselves that our occupation of the West Bank and Gaza was a 'benign' occupation. . . ."

Dr. Newman points out that, "We are becoming the pariah of the world, just as South Africa was during the apartheid era. And if we simplistically attribute it to good old-fashioned anti-Semitism, we are missing the point. Neither President Bush nor [British] Prime Minister Tony Blair can be accused of being anti-Semitic. . . . But they do oppose our continued occupation of the West Bank and Gaza Strip and they do favor the establishment of a Palestinian state alongside the state of Israel. No amount of newspeak or closure of the territories can change these basic facts and any attempt to argue otherwise only blackens our image throughout the world."

It is, of course, easier to silence criticism with charges of anti-Semitism than to confront the complex realities of the Middle East. This is the course many in the organized Jewish community have taken. *New York Times* columnist Thomas Friedman wrote on April 3, 2002, of "the feckless American Jewish leaders" who have "helped to make it impossible for anyone in the U.S. administration to talk seriously about halting Israeli settlement-building without being accused of being anti-Israel. Their collaboration has helped prolong a colonial Israeli occupation that now threatens the entire Zionist enterprise."

Moving toward Middle East peace requires honest debate and discussion on all sides. Those who seek to stifle such debate, it seems, have an agenda other than peace.

8

Israel's Defense of Democratic Ideals Promotes Anti-Semitism

Natan Sharansky

Natan Sharansky was born in the former Soviet Union in 1948. He earned a degree in computer science from the Physical Technical Institute of Moscow. He was jailed by the Soviet government for eleven years for attempting to gain the right for Russian Jews to immigrate to Israel. Freed in 1986, Sharansky immigrated to Israel and now serves in its government as the minister for Jerusalem and Diaspora Affairs.

The Jewish people have always been opposed to tyranny and oppression. By establishing a democracy in an autocratic Middle East, Israel is seen by some people in the Middle East as rejecting the prevailing order. Because it stands for freedom and democratic ideals and because the authoritarian states of the Middle East fear democratic freedoms, Israel, which was founded on the hope of eradicating anti-Semitism, has in fact had the effect of promoting anti-Semitism. Israel shares its search for freedom with the people of the United States, and it also shares the enmity of those who oppose democratic freedoms. Anti-Americanism closely resembles anti-Semitism. Irrational fears about democracy and the Jewish people are at the core of both anti-Semitism and anti-Americanism. These irrational prejudices threaten modern democratic societies, and both Israel and the United States must continue to fight against tyranny for the principles of freedom.

Natan Sharansky, "On Hating the Jews," *Commentary*, vol. 116, November 2003, p. 26. Copyright © 2003 by the American Jewish Committee. Reproduced by permission.

No hatred has as rich and as lethal a history as anti-Semitism —"the longest hatred," as the historian Robert Wistrich has dubbed it. Over the millennia, anti-Semitism has infected a multitude of peoples, religions, and civilizations, in the process inflicting a host of terrors on its Jewish victims. But while there is no disputing the impressive reach of the phenomenon, there is surprisingly little agreement about its cause or causes. . . .

Three decades ago, as a young dissident in the Soviet Union, I compiled underground reports on anti-Semitism for foreign journalists and Western diplomats. At the time, I firmly believed that the cause of the "disease" was totalitarianism, and that democracy was the way to cure it. Once the Soviet regime came to be replaced by democratic rule, I figured, anti-Semitism was bound to wither away. In the struggle toward that goal, the free world, which in the aftermath of the Holocaust appeared to have inoculated itself against a recurrence of murderous anti-Jewish hatred, was our natural ally, the one political entity with both the means and the will to combat the great evil.

> *Zionists . . . believed that the emergence of a Jewish state would end anti-Semitism.*

Today I know better. Following publication of a report by an Israeli government forum charged with addressing the issue of anti-Semitism, I invited to my office the ambassadors of the two countries that have outpaced all others in the frequency and intensity of anti-Jewish attacks within their borders. The emissaries were from France and Belgium—two mature democracies in the heart of Western Europe. It was in these ostensible bastions of enlightenment and tolerance that Jewish cemeteries were being desecrated, children assaulted, synagogues scorched.

To be sure, the anti-Semitism now pervasive in Western Europe is very different from the anti-Semitism I encountered a generation ago in the Soviet Union. In the latter, it was nurtured by systematic, government-imposed discrimination against Jews. In the former, it has largely been condemned and opposed by governments (though far less vigilantly than it should be). But this only makes anti-Semitism in the democracies more disturbing, shattering the illusion—which was hardly mine alone—that representative governance is an infallible antidote to active hatred of Jews.

The Founding of the Jewish State

Another shattered illusion is even more pertinent to our search. Shocked by the visceral anti-Semitism he witnessed at the Dreyfus trial[1] in supposedly enlightened France, Theodor Herzl, the founder of modern Zionism, became convinced that the primary cause of anti-Semitism was the anomalous condition of the Jews: a people without a polity of its own. In his seminal work, *The Jewish State* (1896), published two years after the trial, Herzl envisioned the creation of such a Jewish polity and predicted that a mass emigration to it of European Jews would spell the end of anti-Semitism. Although his seemingly utopian political treatise would turn out to be one of the 20th century's most prescient books, on this point history has not been kind to Herzl; no one would seriously argue today that anti-Semitism came to a halt with the founding of the state of Israel. To the contrary, this particular illusion has come full circle: while Herzl and most Zionists after him believed that the emergence of a Jewish state would end anti-Semitism, an increasing number of people today, including some Jews, are convinced that anti-Semitism will end only with the disappearance of the Jewish state. . . .

The Rise of Extreme Anti-Semitism

Obviously, the state of Israel cannot be the cause of a phenomenon that predates it by over 2,000 years. But might it be properly regarded as the cause of contemporary anti-Semitism? What is certain is that, everywhere one looks, the Jewish state does appear to be at the center of the anti-Semitic storm—and nowhere more so, of course, than in the Middle East.

The rise in viciously anti-Semitic content disseminated through state-run Arab media is quite staggering, and has been thoroughly documented. Arab propagandists, journalists, and scholars now regularly employ the methods and the vocabulary used to demonize European Jews for centuries—calling Jews Christ-killers, charging them with poisoning non-Jews,

---

1. Alfred Dreyfus, an officer in the French army, was falsely tried and convicted of treason in 1894. He was later pardoned. His trial exposed anti-Semitism in the French army.

fabricating blood libels, and the like. In a region where the Christian faith has few adherents, a lurid and time-worn Christian anti-Semitism boasts an enormous following. . . .

In Europe, the connection between Israel and anti-Semitism is equally conspicuous. For one thing, the timing and nature of the attacks on European Jews, whether physical or verbal, have all revolved around Israel, and the anti-Semitic wave itself, which began soon after the Palestinians launched their terrorist campaign against the Jewish state in September 2000, reached a peak (so far) when Israel initiated Operation Defensive Shield at the end of March 2002, a month in which 125 Israelis had been killed by terrorists.

> *Persecution of the powerless Jews was justified as a kind of divine payback for the Jewish rejection of Jesus.*

Though most of the physical attacks in Europe were perpetrated by Muslims, most of the verbal and cultural assaults came from European elites. Thus, the Italian newspaper *La Stampa* published a cartoon of an infant Jesus lying at the foot of an Israeli tank, pleading, "Don't tell me they want to kill me again." The frequent comparisons of [Israeli prime minister] Ariel Sharon to Adolf Hitler, of Israelis to Nazis, and of Palestinians to the Jewish victims of the Holocaust were not the work of hooligans spray-painting graffiti on the wall of a synagogue but of university educators and sophisticated columnists. As the Nobel Prize–winning author Jose Saramago declared of Israel's treatment of the Palestinians: "We can compare it with what happened at Auschwitz.". . .

But if Israel is indeed nothing more than the world's Jew, then to say that the world increasingly hates Jews because the world increasingly hates Israel means as much, or as little, as saying that the world hates Jews because the world hates Jews. We still need to know: why?

Ancient Anti-Semitism

This may be a good juncture to let the anti-Semites speak for themselves.

Here is the reasoning invoked by Haman, the infamous viceroy of Persia in the biblical book of Esther, to convince his king to order the annihilation of the Jews:

> There is a certain people scattered and dispersed among the people in all the provinces of your kingdom, and their laws are different from those of other peoples, and the king's laws they do not keep, so that it is of no benefit for the king to tolerate them. If it please the king, let it be written that they be destroyed.

This is hardly the only ancient source pointing to the Jews' incorrigible separateness, or their rejection of the majority's customs and moral concepts, as the reason for hostility toward them. Centuries after Hellenistic values had spread throughout and beyond the Mediterranean, the Roman historian Tacitus had this to say:

> Among the Jews, all things are profane that we hold sacred; on the other hand, they regard as permissible what seems to us immoral. . . . The rest of the world they confront with the hatred reserved for enemies. They will not feed or intermarry with gentiles. . . . They have introduced circumcision to show that they are different from others. . . . It is a crime among them to kill any newly born infant. . . .

Did the Jews actually reject the values that were dominant in the ancient world, or was this simply a fantasy of their enemies? While many of the allegations leveled at Jews were spurious—they did not ritually slaughter non-Jews, as the Greek writer Apion claimed—some were obviously based on true facts. The Jews did oppose intermarriage. They did refuse to sacrifice to foreign gods. And they did emphatically consider killing a newborn infant to be a crime. . . .

The (by and large correct) perception of the Jews rejecting the prevailing value system of the ancient world hardly justifies the anti-Semitism directed against them; but it does take anti-Semitism out of the realm of fantasy, turning it into a genuine clash of ideals and of values. With the arrival of Christianity on the world stage, that same clash, based once again on the charge of Jewish rejectionism, would intensify a thousandfold. The refusal of the people of the "old covenant" to accept the new came to be defined as a threat to the very legitimacy of Christianity, and one that required a mobilized response.

Branding the Jews "Christ killers" and "sons of devils," the Church launched a systematic campaign to denigrate Christianity's parent religion and its adherents. . . .

According to some Christian thinkers persecution of the powerless Jews was justified as a kind of divine payback for the Jewish rejection of Jesus. This heavenly stamp of approval would be invoked many times through the centuries, especially by those who had tried and failed to convince the Jews to acknowledge the superior truth of Christianity. The most famous case may be that of Martin Luther[2]: at first extremely friendly toward Jews—as a young man he had complained about their mistreatment by the Church—Luther turned into one of their bitterest enemies as soon as he realized that his efforts to woo them to his new form of Christianity would never bear fruit.

Nor was this pattern unique to the Christian religion. Muhammad, too, had hoped to attract the Jewish communities of Arabia, and to this end he initially incorporated elements of Judaism into his new faith (directing prayer toward Jerusalem, fasting on Yom Kippur, and the like). When, however, the Jews refused to accept his code of law, Muhammad wheeled upon them with a vengeance, cursing them in words strikingly reminiscent of the early Church fathers: "Humiliation and wretchedness were stamped upon them, and they were visited with the wrath of Allah. That was because they disbelieved in Allah's revelation and slew the prophets wrongfully."

In these cases, too, we might ask whether the perception of Jewish rejectionism was accurate. Of course the Jews did not drain the blood of children, poison wells, attempt to mutilate the body of Christ, or commit any of the other wild crimes of which the Church accused them. Moreover, since many teachings of Christianity and Islam stemmed directly from Jewish ones, Jews could hardly be said to have denied them. But if rejecting the Christian or Islamic world meant rejecting the Christian or Islamic creed, then Jews who clung to their own separate faith and way of life were, certainly, rejectionist. . . .

On closer inspection, then, modern anti-Semitism begins to look quite continuous with pre-modern anti-Semitism, only worse. Modern Jews may not have believed they were rejecting the prevailing order around them, but that did not necessarily

2. Martin Luther was a sixteenth-century German theologian whose ideas led to the development of the Protestant Church.

mean their enemies agreed with them. When it came to the Jews, indeed, European nationalism of the blood-and-soil variety only added another and even more murderous layer of hatred to the foundation built by age-old religious prejudice. Just as in the ancient world, the Jews in the modern world remained the other—inveterate rejectionists, no matter how separate, no matter how assimilated.

Was there any kernel of factual truth to this charge? It is demeaning to have to point out that, wherever and whenever they were given the chance, most modern Jews strove to become model citizens and showed, if anything, an exemplary talent for acculturation; the idea that by virtue of their birth, race, or religion they were implacable enemies of the state or nation was preposterous. So, too, with other modern libels directed against the Jews, which displayed about as much or as little truth content as ancient ones. The Jews did not and do not control the banks. They did not and do not control the media of communication. They did not and do not control governments, and they are not plotting to take over anything.

What some of them have indeed done, in various places and under specific circumstances, is to demonstrate—with an ardor and tenacity redolent perhaps of their long national experience—an attachment to great causes of one stripe or another, including, at times, the cause of their own people. This has had the effect (not everywhere, of course, but notably in highly stratified and/or intolerant societies) of putting them in a visibly adversary position to prevailing values or ideologies, and thereby awakening the never dormant dragon of anti-Semitism. Particularly instructive in this regard is the case of Soviet Jewry.

Jews in Soviet Russia

What makes the Soviet case instructive is, in no small measure, the fact that the professed purpose of Communism was to abolish all nations, peoples, and religions—those great engines of exclusion—on the road to the creation of a new world and a new man. As is well known, quite a few Jews, hoping to emancipate humanity and to "normalize" their own condition in the process, hitched their fates to this ideology and to the movements associated with it. After the Bolshevik revolution[3]

---

3. The Bolshevik revolution, led by the Communist Vladimir Lenin, took over the Russian government in 1917.

these Jews proved to be among the most devoted servants of the Soviet regime.

Once again, however, the perception of ineradicable Jewish otherness proved as lethal as any reality. In the eyes of [Soviet dictator Joseph] Stalin and his henchmen, the Jews, starting with the loyal Communists among them, were always suspect—"ideological immigrants," in the telling phrase. But the animosity went beyond Jewish Communists. The Soviet regime declared war on the over 100 nationalities and religions under its boot; whole peoples were deported, entire classes destroyed, millions starved to death, and tens of millions killed. Everybody suffered, not only Jews. But, decades later, long after Stalin's repression had given way to [Nikita] Khrushchev's "thaw," only one national language, Hebrew, was still banned in the Soviet Union; only one group, the Jews, was not permitted to establish schools for its children; only in the case of one group, the Jews, did the term "fifth line," referring to the space reserved for nationality on a Soviet citizen's identification papers, become a code for licensed discrimination. . . .

And so we arrive back at today, and at the hatred that takes as its focus the state of Israel. That state—the world's Jew—has the distinction of challenging two separate political/moral orders simultaneously: the order of the Arab and Muslim Middle East, and the order that prevails in Western Europe. The Middle Eastern case is the easier to grasp; the Western European one may be the more ominous.

Anti-Semitism in the Middle East and Europe

The values ascendant in today's Middle East are shaped by two forces: Islamic fundamentalism and state authoritarianism. In the eyes of the former, any non-Muslim sovereign power in the region—for that matter, any secular Muslim power—is anathema. Particularly galling is Jewish sovereignty in an area delineated as dar al-Islam, the realm where Islam is destined to enjoy exclusive dominance. Such a violation cannot be compromised with; nothing will suffice but its extirpation.

In the eyes of the secular Arab regimes, the Jews of Israel are similarly an affront, but not so much on theological grounds as on account of the society they have built: free, productive, democratic, a living rebuke to the corrupt, autocratic regimes surrounding it. In short, the Jewish state is the ultimate freedom fighter—an embodiment of the subversive liberties that threaten Islamic civilization and autocratic Arab rule alike. It is for this reason that in the state-controlled Arab media as in the mosques, Jews have been turned into a symbol of all that is menacing in the democratic, materialist West as a whole, and are confidently reputed to be the insidious force manipulating the United States into a confrontation with Islam.

The particular dynamic of anti-Semitism in the Middle East orbit today may help explain why—unlike, as we shall see, in Europe—there was no drop in the level of anti-Jewish incitement in the region after the inception of the Oslo peace process [1993 Israeli-Palestinian peace agreements]. Quite the contrary. The reason is plain: to the degree that Oslo were to have succeeded in bringing about a real reconciliation with Israel or in facilitating the spread of political freedom, to that degree it would have frustrated the overarching aim of eradicating the Jewish "evil" from the heart of the Middle East and/or preserving the autocratic power of the Arab regimes. . . .

> *Jews have been turned into a symbol of all that is menacing in the democratic, materialist West.*

Before 1967, anti-Zionist resolutions sponsored by the Arabs and their Soviet patrons in the United Nations garnered little or no support among the democracies. After 1967, more and more Western countries joined the chorus of castigation. By 1974, Yasir Arafat, whose organization [the Palestine Liberation Organization] openly embraced both terrorism and the destruction of a UN member state, was invited to address the General Assembly. The next year, that same body passed the infamous "Zionism-is-racism" resolution. In 1981, Israel's strike against Iraq's nuclear reactor was condemned by the entire world, including the United States.

Then, in the 1990's, things began to change again. Despite the constant flow of biased UN resolutions, despite the continuing double standard, there were a number of positive developments as well: the Zionism-is-racism resolution was repealed, and over 65 member states either established or renewed diplomatic relations with Israel. . . .

But of course it would not last. In the summer of 2000, at

Camp David, Ehud Barak offered the Palestinians nearly everything their leadership was thought to be demanding. The offer was summarily rejected, Arafat started his "'uprising," Israel undertook to defend itself—and Europe ceased to applaud. For many Jews at the time, this seemed utterly incomprehensible: had not Israel taken every last step for peace? But it was all too comprehensible. Europe was staying true to form; it was the world's Jew, by refusing to accept its share of blame for the "cycle of violence," that was out of line. And so were the world's Jews, who by definition, and whether they supported Israel or not, came rapidly to be associated with the Jewish state, in its effrontery.

America and Israel

Israel and the Jewish people share something essential with the United States. The Jews, after all, have long held that they were chosen to play a special role in history, to be what their prophets called "a light unto the nations." What precisely is meant by that phrase has always been a matter of debate, and I would be the last to deny the mischief that has sometimes been done, including to the best interests of the Jews, by some who have raised it as their banner. Nevertheless, over four millennia, the universal vision and moral precepts of the Jews have not only worked to secure the survival of the Jewish people themselves but have constituted a powerful force for good in the world, inspiring myriads to fight for the right even as in others they have aroused rivalry, enmity, and unappeasable resentment.

Fortunately for America, and fortunately for the world, the United States has been blessed by providence with the power to match its ideals. The Jewish state, by contrast, is a tiny island in an exceedingly dangerous sea, and its citizens will need every particle of strength they can muster for the trials ahead. It is their own people's astounding perseverance, despite centuries of suffering at the hands of faiths, ideologies, peoples, and individuals who have hated them and set out to do them in, that inspires one with confidence that the Jews will once again outlast their enemies.

9

Anti-Semitism in France Is Increasing

Michel Gurfinkiel

Michel Gurfinkiel, editor in chief of the French weekly Valeurs Actuelles, *is the author of numerous books, including* How to Cook a Lobster: Impertinent Reflections on the Middle East Crisis.

Since the end of World War II in 1945, French Jews, who amount to one percent of the French population, have prospered both culturally and economically. However, this golden age of French Jewry ended in October of 2000 when violent waves of anti-Semitism began sweeping through France. The violent attacks included the burning of synagogues, homes, and businesses. Despite the serious nature of these attacks, French leaders ignored and downplayed the problems. One reason for these attacks is that French society is experiencing a large increase in its Muslim population, which is ten times the size of the Jewish population. While most French Muslims are not anti-Semitic, some are blatantly anti-Semitic. France's resurgence of anti-Semitism is not a reversion to a pre–World War II hatred of the Jews, but rather represents the influx of anti-Semitism fostered by Islamic immigrants.

In 1928, the young New York intellectual Sidney Hook embarked on a tour of Europe that included a stay of several months in Germany. More than a half-century later, he would write in his memoirs, *Out of Step:* "As incredible as it may sound to most people today, anti-Semitism was much less apparent at

Michel Gurfinkiel, "France's Jewish Problem," *Commentary*, vol. 114, July/August 2002, p. 38. Copyright © 2002 by the American Jewish Committee. Reproduced by permission.

the time in Berlin than in New York City." Indeed, in the Weimar Republic that had been established in 1919, both Jews as individuals and the Jewish community as a whole were flourishing; in the United States, by contrast, nativist prejudice in the late 20's was on the rise and free immigration had been sharply curtailed.

It took no more than five years after Hook's visit, however, for Germany to become the most murderously anti-Semitic nation in history. By September 1930, economic depression and mass unemployment had propelled the tiny Nazi party into mainstream politics. By January 1933, Adolf Hitler had become chancellor of the Reich [the German government]; by March 1933, he was firmly entrenched as dictator.

It is always perilous to draw strict parallels in history, and in any case both the Nazi regime and the genocide it engineered—the Holocaust—were exceptional in too many respects to bear recounting. Still, what remains striking in the light of Hook's observation is the sheer rapidity with which Nazi anti-Semitism established itself within a seemingly peaceful and open society. Could such a reversal happen again in a Western nation, even if at a lower and less lethal level? This question, which has haunted many Jews since 1945 and until recently seemed largely theoretical, took on new significance [in 2002] in France.

The 20th Century: Golden Age for French Jewry

The latter half of the 20th century constituted a kind of golden age for French Jewry. A community whose numbers stood at around 300,000 at the end of World War II had by the 1990's increased enormously in size, through both natural growth and immigration from former French colonies in North Africa as well as from elsewhere around the Mediterranean and from Central and Eastern Europe. Although neither religion nor race is recorded in the French census, and although (unlike in Germany) there is no official registration of one's religious affiliation, it is reliably estimated that out of a total population of 60 million Frenchmen, roughly 1 percent, or between 600,000 and 700,000 people, are "fully involved" Jews, and perhaps an additional 200,000 manifest some awareness of Jewish origins or a concern with Jewish affairs. . . .

As it has become easier to lead a Jewish life in France, many Jews have become more traditionalist in their habits and practice. Study groups in Talmud [a collection of ancient Jewish writings] or Jewish thought have burgeoned, and some have evolved into real centers of learning. Distinct Orthodox neighborhoods have grown up in greater Paris as well as in Marseilles, Nice, and Strasbourg; in a number of places, Liberal (Reform) and Conservative congregations have been founded as well. Even secularist Jews have organized themselves here and there in self-conscious efforts to preserve a Jewish way of life. All in all, contemporary French Jewry has begun to look somewhat like American Jewry.

That is in social terms. In political terms, the situation in the two countries is very different. France's is not a federal system, nor is government rooted so thoroughly in electoral politics as is the case in the U.S.; the country is less a "republic" ruled by its citizens than a "state" administered by a professional class of civil servants. Lobbying for special interests, while widespread in fact, is still considered not quite legitimate, and religion- or community-based activism is frowned upon. As a result, although individual Jews have certainly achieved prominence in political life or in the civil service, or both, Jewish groups do not and cannot operate as freely and openly in the pursuit of their political interests as they do in the United States.

This is not to say that the influence of French Jews in public life has been insignificant. With regard to Israel, although it has so far proved impossible to change the frankly pro-Arab stance first charted by Charles de Gaulle in the wake of the Six-Day war of 1967, efforts to mitigate that stance over the decades have met with periodic success. Elsewhere, in matters pertaining to civil rights or religious observance, Holocaust memorials or the prosecution of Nazi criminals, Jewish interests have been readily accommodated. . . .

But as the whole world knows by now, the golden age is over. So sharply and so abruptly has the situation deteriorated that by the end of 2001, Rabbi Michael Melchior, Israel's deputy prime minister, could characterize France as "the most anti-Semitic country in the West." Were there a worldwide Richter scale of anti-Semitism, what has happened in France would qualify as an earthquake.

Anti-Semitic Violence Erupts

On October 3, 2000, the synagogue of Villepinte, a suburban neighborhood in northeastern Paris, was all but destroyed by arson in practically the first such case in France since the late Middle Ages. (The single exception had occurred in 1940 when the Nazis blew up the Central Synagogue of Strasbourg.) Following Villepinte, four more synagogues were burned over the next ten days, all of them in greater Paris, while in the whole of France, nineteen further attempts at arson were recorded against synagogues or other Jewish buildings, homes, or businesses. The week of October 7 also witnessed four incidents of vandalism or desecration, three of them involving synagogues, and eighteen more cases of anti-Jewish violence, from stone-throwing to beating. Most occurred in mixed neighborhoods with both Jewish and Muslim residents, and were connected in some way with the organized riots by Palestinians against Israel that had begun in Jerusalem in late September.

Anti-Jewish violence subsided in France after October 2000 but hardly ceased. It flared up again a year later after the September 11 [2001] terrorist attack on the United States, which generated a wave of pride among French Muslims. A third peak occurred around Passover and Easter of [2002] as the Palestinian intifada [uprising] against Israel turned into open warfare. In Lyons, an anti-Jewish gang used a car equipped with battering rams to smash the doors of a local synagogue and community center and then set the building aflame. In Marseilles, another synagogue was entirely destroyed by arson. In Toulouse, a man opened fire on a kosher butcher shop. At Villeurbanne, near Lyons, an Orthodox couple on their way to prayer were beaten in the street. At Bondy, near Paris, hooded thugs assaulted the local Jewish soccer team and forced it to flee the field. A school bus was stoned by another gang in a new Orthodox neighborhood in Paris, while in the Marais district, at the heart of the old Jewish "Pletzl [neighborhood]" a young man was abducted on his way home from synagogue on Friday night by three Arab immigrants and terrorized for two hours before being released.

Increasing Anti-Semitic Harassment

Physical violence was accompanied by harassment and discrimination. These were particularly noticeable in the public schools, where Jewish pupils and teachers alike were subjected to ostracism and insults. In one by no means isolated incident, a twelve-year-old boy from a secular family was threatened and humiliated by his Arab schoolmates; in another, a Jewish high-school teacher was harassed by students and colleagues and denied help by the principal. All over France, annual "Holocaust-awareness" programs had to be canceled on account of student opposition.

> **/ /** *Were there a worldwide Richter scale of anti-Semitism, what has happened in France would qualify as an earthquake.* **/ /**

Then there was the increasingly open and uninhibited expression of anti-Semitic sentiment. Although no French political party of significant size called for anti-Jewish policies as such, the Green party and related groups on the Left denounced "Jewish religious fundamentalists" and pro-Israel activity. (On the other side of the political spectrum, the far-Right leader Jean-Marie Le Pen had indulged for years in anti-Semitic innuendo, but in the current crisis mostly held his tongue.) At pro-Palestinian rallies, calls to kill the Jews ("Mort aux juifs!") were raised again and again; anti-Jewish invective laced sermons preached in church; and there were anti-Jewish cartoons in the mainstream press. Liberation, a left-of-center newspaper, carried several such cartoons, the most offensive of which, published the day after Christmas 2001, showed Prime Minister Ariel Sharon standing next to a cross with a hammer in his hand and nails in his mouth. The caption: "No Christmas for [Palestinian leader Yasir] Arafat. But he is welcome on Easter." Two days earlier, at midnight mass in Montpellier, a Catholic priest had handed out the text for a hymn in the Occitan language [of Provençal, France,] that read: "He was born in Bethlehem, Palestine. He was born in Bethlehem, poor and innocent. Sharon shot him down. . . ."

France's Exploding Muslim Population

If demographics was the driving force behind the Jewish golden age in the second half of the 20th century, demographics will be seen to have played a major part as well in the rise of French Muslims in the first half of the 21st. The fact is that France itself is undergoing a partial Islamicization. The Muslim population, already ten times the size of the Jewish community, is growing rapidly, and the thorough transformation it is wreaking in France's ethnic and religious fabric obviously has much to do both with the increase in anti-Semitism and with the official denial of it.

The modern Muslim community in France stems ultimately from the country's various overseas colonies, the protectorates or mandates of Algeria, Tunisia, the Sahara and West Africa, Morocco, Syria, and Lebanon. Inevitably, the more Islamic lands the French added to their empire, the more Muslims settled in France proper. A turning point was World War I, when 300,000 Muslims from the Maghreb [northwest Africa] were drafted to fight or otherwise aid the war effort, one third of whom stayed in the country after the war. In 1920 the French parliament passed a special law to fund a Great Mosque in Paris (notwithstanding the 1905 law separating church and state). By the late 50's and early 60's, when the empire dissolved, a Muslim population of a half-million was in place. . . .

In 1995, an authoritative report in *Le Monde* gave a figure of three to four million Muslims in France. In the wake of the 2002 presidential and parliamentary elections, the accepted figure has been raised to about six million, or fully 10 percent of the population. Such a dramatic increase—50 percent in under ten years—would suggest either that the earlier figures were much too conservative or that illegal immigration has reached unprecedented levels. Some demographers, moreover, think that the true number may be closer to seven or even eight million. . . .

To be sure, a fair number of French Muslims have integrated into mainstream society, just like immigrant groups before them. Some of these "republican Muslims" insist on being regarded as French citizens plain and simple, while others embrace a hyphenated (French-Muslim, or French-Arab, or French-Berber) identity. Most also reject anti-Semitism and take pride in the age-old kinship between Islam and Judaism. Ali Magoudi, a psychoanalyst, has written extensively about the Holocaust; Malek Boutih, a left-of-center leader of the group SOS Racisme, extended open support to the Jewish community throughout the current cycle of violence; Zair Kedadouche and Hamid Lafrad, elected Conservative officials, were no less outspoken in this respect.

But a much larger part of the Muslim community is not integrating at all. Rather, it is turning into a "separatist" underclass that owes exclusive allegiance to Islam and to the Islamic nations—a circumstance that was highlighted last fall [2001] when a largely French-Muslim crowd booed the Marseillaise [French national anthem] at a France-Algeria soccer match. These Muslims also tend to be rabid, unreconstructed anti-Semites, after the fashion of the countries from which they have come. For them, anti-Semitism is a daily staple, to which the Middle East conflict and the saga of [terrorist leader] Osama bin Laden have added more zest.

Between the relatively few Gallicized or "republican" Muslims and the much larger underclass, there is a third, more ambiguous group who are socially and politically quite well integrated but still tend to embrace an all-Muslim ideology; who may frown on anti-Semitism, especially when directed at synagogue-going Jews, but nevertheless indulge in extremist rhetoric when it comes to Israel and the Middle East. Soheir Bencheikh, the self-styled Grand Mufti [Muslim leader] of Marseilles, has for instance simultaneously condemned anti-Jewish violence and defended French Muslim "solidarity with a Palestinian people . . . murdered day after day by blood-thirsty and revanchist Israeli leaders."

The Influence of Muslims on French Politics

It is perilous enough that French Jews are confronted with a group so quickly expanding and so largely hostile. But the collateral effects are even worse. Rational debate about the Israeli-Arab conflict or the terrorist threat cannot easily be conducted in a country where some 10 percent of the population and a larger percentage of young people identify with the most radical elements in the Arab/Islamic world. Moreover, extremist Muslims tend to ally themselves with other extremist groups Left and Right, and thus to bring size, breadth, and market potential to a whole subculture of delusion and fanaticism. Today's runaway best-seller in France is Thierry Meyssan's *The Awful Scare*, whose thesis is that what we saw on television . . . September 11 [2001] was a hoax, carefully staged by American rightists and the Israeli Mossad [intelligence agency]. Similarly, both hard-core anti-Semitism and Holocaust denial, marginal phenomena until very recently, have gained traction thanks to the candid espousal of such themes by Muslims. In the words of the political scientist Frederic Encel, "What is an average French teacher to do when 70 percent of the class object to a course in religious tolerance giving Judaism its proper due, or simply refuse to attend a discussion about the Holocaust on the grounds that it is a Zionist lie?" The answer: "More often than not, he or she drops the matter altogether.". . .

French politics and French society may not be anti-Semitic if considered as a whole, but anti-Jewish symptoms are unmistakably growing in number and intensity, and serious countermeasures are called for.

That, basically, is how French Jews have been reacting since October 2000. They do not say, or for the most part think, that France is the reincarnation of the Third Reich. But they wonder about their future. Applications for immigration to Israel are on the rise, as also for North America (Canada as well as the U.S.). There may also be some movement from France to other European Union countries, especially Britain and Germany, although among those thinking of leaving the prevailing view is that all of Europe is dangerous territory.

Those not contemplating emigration are engaged in soulsearching. No fewer than six major books, by Jewish and non-Jewish authors, have appeared over the last six months [January–July 2002] on French "Judeophobia," and each of them is selling briskly. At synagogues and community centers, in the Jewish media, the future of France and of French Jewry is a constant topic of discussion. . . .

My own first glimpse of things to come occurred on a visit to the Anne Frank House in Amsterdam as long ago as 1977. Anne Frank is an icon of the second approach to the Holocaust: a Jew, but at the same time so convincingly German-Dutch, so "universal," that any child in the world can identify with her. When I was there, the tour ended at a wall bearing premonitory messages about "new Holocausts in the making." One of these messages warned darkly of the consequences of the electoral victory in Israel, a few weeks earlier, of "Menachem Begin's far-Right Likud party."

The present anti-Semitic crisis in France should not be construed as a repetition of the past but rather as a thoroughly modern or, one might say, postmodern or postliberal development. France is not "racist" in the neo-Nazi or Ku Klux Klan sense of that word. But it is on the front line of what [professor] Samuel Huntington has termed the clash of civilizations, and both politically and culturally it is especially ill-equipped to deal with it.

10

Charges of European Anti-Semitism Are Exaggerated

Elliot Neaman

Elliot Neaman, associate professor of history at the University of San Francisco, is the author of A Dubious Past: Ernst Junger and the Politics of Literature After Nazism.

Some people fear that the increasing nationalistic, anti-immigrant, and anti-Israel stance that European leaders have taken in recent years is an ominous sign that Europe is becoming anti-Semitic. Yet, besides the United States, Germany remains Israel's most important economic and military ally. In Germany, criticism of Israel's treatment of the Palestinians is actually part of a wider debate of issues that include the Holocaust, Germany's Nazi past and the Palestinian-Israeli conflict. This vigorous and open debate is evidence of the healthy condition of democracies that exist in Europe today. Free and open debate is the best antidote to fascism, racism and anti-Semitism. Vigorous democratic debate provides strong evidence that European governments are not turning back toward the fascism and anti-Semitism that were a part of their past.

It is by now obvious that the only reason the Bush administration became actively engaged in the Israeli-Palestinian conflict in the spring of 2002 was because the so-called "War on Terror" had brushed up against insurmountable obstacles that required a reorientation of U.S. foreign policy. One of these ob-

Elliot Neaman, "European Right-Wing Populism and Anti-Semitism," *Tikkun*, vol. 17, July/August 2002, p. 53. Copyright © 2002 by *Tikkun*: A Bimonthly Jewish Critique of Politics, Culture & Society. Reproduced by permission.

stacles was that world opinion had shifted to a starkly critical stance towards Israel after the [Israeli prime minister Ariel] Sharon government responded to relentless homicide bomb- ings by occupying six major cities in the West Bank [a Palestin- ian territory] in March and keeping [Palestinian leader Yasir] Arafat under house arrest at his compound in Ramallah [a West Bank city]. Not only on the proverbial "Arab street" but also at the United Nations, and in Europe, the plight of the Palestini- ans seemed to evoke more sympathy than for the Israelis, who had endured a rising number of ruthless attacks on civilians.

In the United States, American Jews became particularly sensitive to any critique of Israel because of the impression made in the media here that the United States was just about Israel's last friend on earth. For example, Paul Wolfowitz, a Bush administration hawk, whose father's family died in the Holocaust, was jeered at a pro-Israel rally in March for stating that Palestinians as well as Israelis had suffered during the in- tifada [Palestinian uprising against Israel].

> *The current rise of right-wing populism cannot be fundamentally attributed to anti-Semitism or anti-Zionism.*

The news from Europe seemed particularly disturbing. In France, the elections for the powerful office of president turned out to be a run-off between the nationalist-conservative incum- bent [President Jacques] Chirac and the neo-fascist (as was la- beled) Jean-Marie Le Pen. In the final vote a popular front from left to center joined together to give Chirac an 82 percent vic- tory. One was reminded of the German presidential election of 1932 when the almost senile Prussian nationalist Paul Von Hin- denburg won as the lesser of two evils against Hitler. In France and elsewhere synagogues were attacked and Jewish gravestones defaced. The reaction here to these events, understandably, was a general fear that European anti-Semitism, never far below the surface, was rearing its ugly head again. But the reaction bor- dered on hysteria. In a satirical but revealing *Saturday Night Live* [American TV comedy show] sketch, a film of typical French scenes rolled, vineyards, cafes, cobblestone streets, the Louvre, while a voice-over declared:

> France, home of the world's greatest painters, chefs and anti-Semites. The French, cowardly, yet opinionated, arrogant, yet foul-smelling, anti-Israel, anti-American and, of course, as always, Jew-hating. . . . With all that is going on in the world, isn't it about time we got back to hating the French?

Anyone with a rudimentary knowledge of European history cannot deny that anti-Semitism has always been part of occidental Christian culture—it presumably always will be as long as Europe resists multiculturalism beyond the current lip service given to that social ideal. But to state the obvious, European nations were not founded by waves of immigrants and thus we cannot expect them to be shaped by pluralism in the American mold. But the current rise of right-wing populism cannot be fundamentally attributed to anti-Semitism or anti-Zionism (which are sometimes, but not always, the same thing).

In three short years, Europe has moved decidedly to the right. In 1999, Social Democrats had a lopsided 13 to 2 majority in the European Council of Ministers (the two were Ireland and Spain). Today, middle-right governments rule in Portugal, Spain, Iceland, Italy, and Norway, while France, Germany, Switzerland, Denmark, Austria, Belgium, and the Netherlands have strong right-wing populist parties (winning between 10 to 20 percent in recent national elections).

The Question of Immigrants in European Society

What has caused this shift? I would argue that Social Democrats (or what we would call "liberals" in the United States) have not paid attention to the real issues that concern middle-class voters. Social democracy was born out of opposition to capitalism, and although that stance has been modified over the years, the European bourgeoisie has become alienated by its anti-bourgeois undertone, its support of ubiquitous state regulation, and its dogmatic moralism in foreign policy issues. The middle classes are also put off by a kind of political correctness that forbids people of "progressive" views to talk about their fears—rising drug use and crime in the cities, the breakdown of families, the relentless commodification of all spheres of life (globalization), and above all, the problems of integrating foreigners into European society. As has been pointed out often in these pages, one of the failings of the modern left in

Western societies is its denigration of ordinary people's hunger for cultural, spiritual, and social meaning in a disenchanted world, where technological gadgets count as progress, gated housing projects are sold as community, and endless consumption is marketed as spiritual satisfaction. The European Right has all the wrong answers to these problems. Instead of speaking honestly, right-wing politicians play a dangerous game, invoking nationalism, a mythical past, and homogeneous cultural identity as a feel-good panacea for their voters.

The politicization of the immigration issue is the most sensitive for Jews, because it can plausibly be seen as a litmus test of the limits of tolerance in European societies. But a closer look at the right-wing populists who have raised this banner on their platform very successfully shows that the picture is more complicated than it appears—and has little to do with anti-Jewish sentiment. The Dutch Populist and former Marxist Pim Fortuyn, who was assassinated by a possibly deranged animal rights activist in May [2002] spoke out bluntly about what many Dutch thought but felt uncomfortable saying aloud— namely that many Muslim immigrants refuse to make any accommodations and are hostile to the liberal openness of Dutch culture, while insisting on receiving the welfare benefits of the state. While one may question the accuracy of Fortuyn's depiction of Muslim intransigence, it is certainly a proper topic for political debate in a once homogeneous society that suddenly finds itself with a ten-percent Muslim population. In any event, this debate about Muslims has little to do with attitudes towards Jews. In fact Jean-Marie Le Pen, who has made anti-Semitic remarks in the past, appealed with some success to the Jewish vote in the last French presidential election by playing the law and order card.

Israel's Partner and Critic

I now turn finally to the case of Germany, where for obvious reasons the declining fortunes of the Left, the resurgence of right-wing populism, a conservative backlash, and suddenly outspoken criticism of Israel portends potentially disturbing political changes. Although the German right has tended, since 1945, to remain on the margins of German political life, from time to time neo-fascist parties have surged in popularity at the local level, but have never overcome the 5 percent clause to gain entry to the German parliament. The recent success of

right-wing parties in East Germany, and of a new "law and order Party" in the West, seems to be a repeat of past successes
based on protest votes against the establishment. The German
elections in the fall of 2002 are going to be very close and [Ed-
mund] Stoiber, the candidate of the conservative Christian
Democrats, would be, if he wins, the most nationalist, most
conservative chancellor since the Weimar republic.[1] But there
are some interesting twists to this story. Since [Konrad] Ade-
nauer, the first postwar chancellor, the relationship between Israel and Germany has been based on active reconciliation,
which culminated in his 1960 meeting with [David] Ben Gu-
rion [Israel's first prime minister]. The Christian Democrats
bound Germany to Israel to demonstrate loyalty to the West
during the Cold War, and out of a desire—at once authentic
and self-serving—to make amends for the horrors of Nazism.
The result was that except for the United States, Germany became Israel's most important military and economic partner in
the entire world. It was the German Left, particularly the
youthful New Left of the 1960s that was hostile to Israel, con-
flating what it saw as an anti-fascist fight against imperialism
with a fight against Zionism.

> **❝** *Inflammatory statements [made about Israel]
> . . . caused a huge furor in Germany and the
> politicians who made them [in the 2002 elections]
> had to go to great lengths to defend themselves
> against . . . charges of anti-Semitism.* **❞**

Today the most important defender of Israel among German politicians is Joshka Fischer, a leading member of the Generation of 1968, who has clashed with his own party, the
Greens, over his declarations of absolute solidarity with Israel
and his criticisms of Arafat. The current wave of criticism
against Israel, by contrast, is now coming from the Christian
Democrats and the Liberals (who unlike American liberals are
free market libertarians). As examples, the Liberal politician Jur-
gen Molleman declared that if he were a Palestinian he would
resist Occupation with any means necessary, and the Christian

---

1. Stoiber did not win the 2002 elections.

Democrat Norbert Blum compared Israel's military actions to a war of destruction—using the Nazi term *Vernichtungskrieg* [war of extermination]. Karl Lamers, of the same party, accused Israel of state terrorism.

What is one to make of these inflammatory statements? First, it should be noted that these remarks caused a huge furor in Germany and the politicians who made them had to go to great lengths to defend themselves against the charges of anti-Semitism. Second, no matter how polemical these statements may appear, they reflect the fact that in Germany a dynamic public sphere exists in which both citizens and politicians engage in serious, usually well-informed debate about crucial issues of the day. Unlike in the United States, where the media is owned by a few large corporations and at least on the issue of Israel are numbingly conformist, political debates in Germany reflect genuinely contrasting viewpoints.

Germany Debates the Holocaust and Its Nazi Past

Finally, it is often said here that the Europeans are happy to see Israel in the role of aggressor because the historical guilt of the crimes of the Holocaust are somehow lessened if Jews themselves can be found guilty of war atrocities. Although certainly some *schadenfreude*[2] is felt by Germans who are tired of apologizing for the past, I find this explanation for the new openness with which Israel is criticized to be unsatisfactory. It is true that many Germans would like to see an end to public discussions about the crimes of the Nazis (one third in a recent poll) and some 20 percent of Germans believe that Jews exploit the guilty feelings of Germans for self-advantage. But these sentiments are normal in a society where the current Germans coming of age are already the third generation with no living connection to the crimes of the Nazi past. One can also turn the numbers quoted above around—two thirds of Germans believe that public discourse on Nazi history should continue. A recent, heated debate erupted about the propriety of novelists in Germany writing about the Nazi period from the point of view of the sufferings of Germans, for example the experience of living through the firebombing of German cities or the persecution of millions of German refugees who had to flee Eastern Europe in the aftermath of the war. Al-

2. a German word that means "a malicious satisfaction in the sufferings of others"

though many stupid things are said in this context, such as the novelist Martin Walser's comment in 1998 that Germans are tired of being beaten over the head with the "Auschwitz club," ordinary Germans did suffer during World War II, a fact that in no way minimalizes Jewish suffering, but is a perfectly legitimate object of historical and literary representation.

Of course one must not be sanguine about the recent eruption of anti-Semitism in Europe. When Jews are attacked by right-wing thugs, as has happened all over Europe [in the spring of 2002], when editorials and cartoons in major European newspapers castigate Israel, and intellectuals pontificate about the actions of the Israeli army while remaining mute about Palestinian terrorism, when Jewish neighborhoods are defaced by graffiti and Jews become fearful for their lives, one cannot say that business is usual. One must always be vigilant when attacks against Jews rise in so-called civilized societies, not only for the obvious reasons, but also because open aggression against Jews may signal other shifts in the political geography. Are we witnessing, for example, a general disintegration of the liberal center in Europe, a harbinger of nationalist authoritarianism or worse, as happened during the interwar period of the 1930s? I don't believe that is the case, but no one can predict the future based on the past. Only by understanding the genuine causes of the attractions of right-wing politics can one hope to defend against its excesses.

Stereotypes die hard. Some seem to reside in the mind of Americans as wartime clichés: the Germans as incorrigible Jew-haters, eternal Nazis, the French Catholics as bigots and Vichy collaborators, the Italians as black-shirted Fascist thugs marching on Rome behind [Fascist dictator Benito] Mussolini. The corollary to the European anti-Semite delighting over images of Palestinians being beaten on television is the American who views every sign of anti-Semitism in Europe as confirmation of the deepest suspicions. But European states have evolved into strong democracies in which the legacy of anti-democracy always plays some role in current politics. The passions aroused by the Mideast conflict are proof of that. As much as some Europeans wish that those painful years of Fascist (and Communist) tyrannies would pass into the past, the collective memory was formed by those events and will not disappear without leaving deep traces. As [Danish philosopher Søren] Kierkegaard once said, life must be lived forwards, but can only be understood backwards.

11

Europeans Shaped the Fanatical Anti-Semitism of Militant Muslims

Richard Webster

Richard Webster, British essayist, author, and scholar, is the author of A Brief History of Blasphemy: Liberalism, Censorship, and the "Satanic Verses."

Anti-Semitism did not originate in the Muslim world. It was imported to the Middle East by Europeans in the early twentieth century. The British and the French transmitted their anti-Semitism to the region when they colonized the Middle East in 1918. During the 1930s, Germany, very influential in the Arab world, launched an anti-Semitic propaganda campaign against the Jewish colony in Palestine. After World War II, Egyptian President Gamal Abde Nasser and Egypt's radical political party, the Muslim Brotherhood, continued to spread anti-Semitic propaganda. The Muslim Brotherhood has been one of the primary influences on the thinking of today's Muslim extremists. The situation worsened in the Middle East when the British promoted a Jewish colony in Palestine that evicted the indigenous population of Palestinians and took their land to establish the state of Israel. The root cause of anti-Semitism in the Middle East can be found in the history of that region, especially in Palestine. Without a solution to the conflict between the Palestinians and the Israelis, anti-Semitism can only increase in the Middle East.

A s this article appears [in December 2002], tens of millions of Muslims throughout the Arab world have almost finished marking the holy month of Ramadan in the manner that has now become customary. Not only have they been fasting from dawn to dusk, but they have also been watching a great deal of television. This year, a 41-part series shown during Ramadan has ignited international controversy.

Knight Without a Horse tells how in 1906 an Egyptian, fighting the British occupation, stumbles on a document that reveals an international Jewish conspiracy for global domination. The document is none other than the Protocols of the Elders of Zion. Although this was long ago exposed in the West as a 19th-century anti-Semitic forgery, created by the Russian secret police, the TV drama treats it as genuine.

The series went ahead despite international protests, thus strengthening the arguments of those who, like [writers] Christopher Hitchens on the left and Andrew Sullivan on the right, have portrayed militant Islam as the new fascism. "Fanatical anti-Semitism," Sullivan has written, ". . . is . . . the acrid glue that unites Saddam, Arafat, al-Qaeda, Hezbollah, Iran and the Saudis. They all hate the Jews and want to see them destroyed."

Is it true that extremist Islam is inherently anti-Semitic? My impression is that this question tends to be avoided (or at least not adequately addressed) by the commentators, such as John Pilger, Robert Fisk and Noam Chomsky, who have written most critically about the war on terrorism. If so, the omission is dangerous, for it leaves extraordinarily powerful ammunition in the sole possession of those who are the advocates of war. Those advocates sometimes seem, on this issue, to be seeing reality more clearly than their opponents do.

The case of [Arab terrorist] Osama Bin Laden is itself instructive. In interviews that he gave before [the terrorist attacks of] 11 September [2001], he made it clear that the jihad he supports is directed against a shadowy alliance of "Jews and crusaders". America is a target because he sees it as the puppet of the Jews. The leaders in America, Bin Laden said, "have fallen victim to Jewish Zionist blackmail." Inside the Pentagon and the CIA [Central Intelligence Agency], "the Jews have the upper hand. . . . They make use of America to further their plans for the world, especially the Islamic world."

Bin Laden's world-view here echoes that of the protocols. The forged document's pervasive influence in the Muslim world is nothing new. Egypt's President [Gamal Abdel] Nasser used it in his war against Israel. King Faisal of Saudi Arabia would present visiting diplomats (including [U.S. secretary of state] Henry Kissinger) with a copy. The Palestinian group Hamas invokes the protocols in its charter. At its worst, extremist Islamic discourse depicts the Jewish people not only as the enemies of [Arab prophet of Islam] Muhammad, but as the friends and allies of Satan.

One reason we hear so little about Arab and Muslim anti-Semitism, except from pro-Israeli commentators, is that it may seem unjust to accuse of vilifying their enemies the very group of people who are among the most vilified in the world: leading Israeli politicians have described the Palestinians as "cockroaches in a glass jar", "two-legged beasts", "lice" and a "cancer".

No less importantly, some commentators and pressure groups have used the charge of anti-Semitism in an attempt to silence journalists who make legitimate criticisms of the Israeli government or military. So frequently have pro-Israeli factions cried wolf in this fashion that they have made it easier for Palestinians and their sympathisers to exploit the mythology of anti-Semitism without attracting censure from western liberals. Yet demonological anti-Semitism, which is almost a religion in itself, remains essentially destructive, however seemingly just the cause in which it is deployed. To demonise your enemy is to confuse issues, destroy moral judgement and block rational analysis. Such demonisation, which invisibly justifies terrible acts of destruction, will poison and corrupt any cause; we have seen the results in the mutilated bodies of Israelis blown up by suicide bombers, in the mass slaughters in Manhattan and Bali. As [Latin American writer and social activist] Eduardo Galeano has written, "In the battle between good and evil it is always the people who get killed."

Anti-Semitism Was Brought to the Middle East by Europeans

But the argument about demonisation cuts both ways. Rather than anathematising Islamic terrorists as "evil", one of the questions we should be asking is why anti-Semitism has taken root within Islam. For demonological anti-Semitism is not an Islamic tradition; it is a specifically western, Christian invention, of which the racial anti-Semitism that emerged at the end of the 19th century was simply a secularised version. "Possibly," wrote the theologian Rosemary Ruether, "anti-Judaism is too deeply embedded in the foundations of Christianity to be rooted out entirely without destroying the whole structure." But whereas Christianity, from the Gospel of John onward, always placed the Jews, as Christ-killers, at the very heart of its demonology, Islam, while revering Jesus as a prophet, actually rejects the view that Jesus was crucified. This does not mean that Islam has been immune to anti-Jewish prejudice. At times, Muslims have subjected Jews to discrimination and persecution. But Islam has never, until recently, showed signs of succumbing to the kind of demonological Jew-hatred that has been endemic in so many versions of Christianity.

> **//** *The destructive form that anti-Semitism has now assumed within militant Islam is not . . . Islamic at all in its origins; it is quintessentially Western.* **//**

It was not until around 1900, with the growing influence of Europeans in the Middle East, and with the active dissemination of anti-Semitism by European colonists, that extreme anti-Semitism spread both among Arab Christians and among Muslims. Western, and particularly British, support for a Zionist [Jewish] state in Palestine made such bigotry more appealing.

The creation of a Jewish homeland in the Middle East was, in part at least, itself an anti-Semitic project. In 1905 (when he was prime minister [of England]), Arthur Balfour (whose declaration of 1917 supported the creation of a Jewish homeland) himself had introduced the Aliens Bill to limit Jewish immigration to Britain. Later, having met and talked to Cosima Wagner [wife of composer Richard Wagner], he confessed to sharing many of her anti-Semitic views. The only Jewish member of the British cabinet at the time of the Balfour Declaration, Edwin Samuel Montagu, opposed it: "The policy of His Majesty's Government," he wrote, "is anti-Semitic . . . and will prove a rallying ground for anti-Semites in every country of the world."

Anti-Semitism in the Arab World

Montagu may never have anticipated the extent to which European anti-Semitism, having played such a significant role in providing the new Zionist colony with its population, would be adopted by Palestinian Arabs. Yet from the 1920s onward, this is what happened. At first, the Grand Mufti of Jerusalem [leader of the Palestinians], Haj Amin al-Husseini, tried to rally both the Muslim masses and Islamic leaders by claiming that the Zionists intended to rebuild Solomon's temples on the ruins of the great mosques. Then during the 1930s, a large part of the Arab world was naturally drawn towards Germany. The Middle East had in effect been taken over by Britain and France since 1918. Now, Germany, which had itself been humiliated by the Treaty of Versailles [World War I peace treaty] seemed ready to humiliate the humiliators. German anti-Semitic propaganda almost immediately began to be used by Arab campaigners against the Zionist colony, which British anti-Semitism had helped to establish. Throughout the war, Haj Amin remained in touch with the Germans, and in 1941, having fled to Berlin, he held talks with Hitler in which he thanked him for the "unequivocal support" he had shown for the Palestinians. Anti-Semitic propaganda broadcast in Arabic from Berlin had a significant effect in Egypt, Iraq, Morocco, Tunisia and other Arab countries.

> *By underwriting a Jewish colony in Palestine, . . . we created in the Middle East a cauldron of hatred.*

Although such propaganda disappeared from Europe after the end of the war, it continued to circulate in the Arab world. In Egypt, anti-Semitism was taken up not only by Nasser, but also, in a particularly violent form, by Sayyid Qutb, the western-influenced ideologue of the Muslim Brotherhood [political party] whom Nasser executed and who more than anyone else shaped the thinking of modern, militant Islam, including that of Bin Laden. In Qutb's view, Jews, who had always rebelled against God, were inherently evil: "From such creatures who kill, massacre and defame prophets, one can only expect the spilling of human blood and dirty means which would further their machinations and evilness."

The destructive form that anti-Semitism has now assumed within militant Islam is not, therefore, Islamic at all in its origins; it is quintessentially Western. Certainly, the dreams of world domination which drive radical Islamists have been there from the beginning. But neither those dreams nor their violent righteousness are unique to Islam. They are the common property of all three Abrahamic faiths; Judaism, Christianity and Islam have always been, at their scriptural core, ideologies of world domination. It was in the Christian tradition alone that the fantasy of world domination was denied and projected on to the Jewish people. This is why it is simplistic to refer, as Hitchens has done, to "fascism with an Islamic face". By using this formula, Hitchens—like George Bush announcing a war against "evil"—intensifies the progressive demonisation of radical Islam, which has been going on for many years. And Hitchens's solution is as chilling as that of the Arab anti-Semites. "It is impossible," he writes, "to compromise with proponents of sacrificial killing of civilians, with the disseminators of anti-Semitic filth, with the violators of women and the cheerful murderers of children . . . In confronting such people, the crucial thing is to be willing and able, if not in fact eager, to kill them without pity before they can get started."

The Creation of Israel Fosters Anti-Semitism

Those on the right who have taken up the chant of "Islamofascism" repeatedly enjoin us to "forget the root causes". Yet the point of the military and political decisions being taken now is to eliminate or lessen the perils facing us. If we ignore history in doing this, we may increase those perils. We should recognise that the direct responsibility for the transfer of a murderous form of anti-Semitism from Christianity to Islam lies with the decision of the great powers, and above all of Britain, to back the Zionist project.

> *By embracing extreme forms of anti-Semitism which are un-Islamic, . . . [militant Islam] has assisted its own demonisation.*

By underwriting a Jewish colony in Palestine, whose continued existence depended upon evicting Palestinians from their homes, expropriating their land and ruthlessly crushing any resistance, we created in the Middle East a cauldron of hatred. In conferring statehood upon this colony and in watching silently, or with insufficient protests, as the artificial Jewish nation became an expansionist power, enforcing its colonial designs by war, by the application of terror against civilians, by bullying and intimidation or by "targeted killings", we have allowed that hatred to deepen inexorably. And by failing to recognise the extent to which, over a period of almost a century, the poison of western anti-Semitism was being stirred into this deadly brew and disseminated throughout the Middle East and beyond, we have produced one of the most lethal conflicts in history.

Militant Islam Embraces Terror

What makes the conflict so dangerous is that the creation of the state of Israel overlapped with the establishment throughout the Middle East of western-led or western-inspired regimes that set out to marginalise or crush traditional religious observance. In Egypt, in Tunisia, in Iran and elsewhere, such secularist regimes enraged devout Muslims. In Iran, for example, Britain and America directly sponsored the regimes of two westernising tyrants, the Shah and his father, who used torture and terror in their efforts to undermine ordinary Muslim piety. The result was a brutal Islamic revolution that unleashed anti-Israeli and anti-American terrorism on an unprecedented scale.

Militant Islam has now provided America with the perfect justification to intensify the policy of world domination it has long pursued. By adopting a strategy of murderous terror and by striking principally against American citizens, it has enabled the US to make its imperial ambitions seem reasonable. By embracing extreme forms of anti-Semitism which are un-Islamic, and a medieval form of sharia [Muslim religious] law that is not supported by millions of moderate Muslims, it has assisted its own demonisation. A US foreign policy strategy—many elements of which were formulated before 11 September, and which would once have aroused substantial opposition even inside America—has been made to appear ethically respectable.

Hitchens, the quondam [sometime] leftist, and Sullivan, the Catholic Republican, stress the repressiveness of radical Islam, its misogyny, its anti-Semitism and its religious dreams of world domination. A grasp of these is essential to any understanding of our present predicament. Yet they have often been absent from the left's analysis of 11 September and its aftermath. The danger of this omission is that Hitchens, Sullivan and all those commentators who have characterised their opponents as "Islamofascist" are currently succeeding in persuading many people of what is false by urging upon them what is true. Contrary to what they suggest, the greatest threat to world peace is not that posed by Islamist dreams of world domination. It is that posed by the corresponding American dreams, which are much nearer to being realised, but which, precisely because the imperialism of the United States is the habitual environment in which we live, have been rendered, like the ocean to the fish, all but invisible to us.

The idea that there is some kind of autonomous "Islamofascism" that can be crushed, or that the west may defend itself against the terrorists who threaten it by cultivating that eagerness to kill militant Muslims which Hitchens urges upon us, is a dangerous delusion. The symptoms that have led some to apply the label of "Islamofascism" are not reasons to forget root causes. They are reasons for us to examine even more carefully what those root causes actually are.

When we do so, we find that the key to the problem remains in the history of western colonialism in the Middle East, and above all in Palestine. It is there, and not in Iraq or Iran or Syria, that our main political energies and our strategic intelligence should now be deployed.

12

Some Muslims Reject Anti-Semitism

Yigal Carmon

Yigal Carmon, terrorism adviser to Israeli prime ministers Yitzhak Shamir and Yitzhak Rabin, is president of the Middle East Media Research Institute, a nonprofit organization that translates Arabic-language news articles and broadcasts for Western audiences.

In recent years Arab writers and politicians have openly criticized anti-Semitic statements made in the Arab media. Often Arab denouncements of anti-Semitism come in response to criticism by Western leaders like President George W. Bush and members of the U.S. Congress, who have read translations of racist articles published in the Arab press and have pressured Middle Eastern leaders to stop promoting anti-Semitic propaganda. Many Arab writers, however, have refuted anti-Semitic statements on the grounds that they are false and inhuman, while others have rejected anti-Semitism for practical reasons, realizing that promoting anti-Jewish stereotypes only harms the image of Arabs in the eyes of the rest of the world.

In the past, manifestations of antisemitism in the Arab world aroused no domestic criticism to speak of. Moreover, Western criticism of antisemitism only increased antisemitic statements in the Arab press, and sparked no rethinking. For example, the February 1998 conviction of French Holocaust denier Roger Garaudy and the March 2000 conviction of British Holocaust denier David Irving enraged the Arab world and brought about increased Holocaust denial in the Arab world, along with greater insistence that Jews had cast their hegemony on the entire world.

[Since 2001], however, the Arab media has reflected significant criticism of, and reservations regarding, manifestations of antisemitism in the Arab world. The following are noteworthy examples of this kind of reaction in the Arab media, and a discussion of their causes and characteristics.

Calls to Cancel the Beirut Holocaust Deniers' Conference

An international conference of Holocaust deniers had been planned for late March 2001, in Beirut. Organizing the conference were the Los Angeles–based Institute for Historical Review and the Swiss organization Verité et Justice. Arab intellectuals opposed to the conference called for canceling it. A communiqué issued by 14 well-known Arab intellectuals read in part: "Arab intellectuals are outraged by this antisemitic undertaking. We wish to warn Lebanese and Arab public opinion about this and call on Lebanese authorities to ban this inadmissible conference."

The communiqué was signed by the Lebanese poet Adonis, the Palestinian poet Mahmoud Darwish, the Algerian historian Muhammad Harabi, Algerian author Jamal Al-Din ibn Sheikh, Moroccan author Muhammad Baradeh, and the Lebanese authors Dominic Awdeh, Elias Khouri, Gerard Khouri, and Salah Sathithiyyeh, as well as Syrian authors Fayez Mallas and Farouq Mardam-Bey, Palestinian authors Khalda Said and Elias Sanbar, and Palestinian-American academic Edward Said.

In an article titled "The Protocols of the Elders of Beirut," columnist Joseph Samaha wrote in the Arabic-language London daily *Al-Hayat:* "Holding the conference in Beirut brings no honor to the Lebanese capital. Perhaps its conceptual, political, and economic damage are inestimably greater than its benefit, which from the outset was nearly nonexistent. The conference will convene forgers of history who have stood trial in their own countries. This is, in effect, a conference against the truth. . . . This is a conference against consciousness. . . ."

"The conference defends the Nazi hangman and his crime against the Jews and others, in the name of the Palestinian and Arab victim. This is a Western-Western settling of accounts, in which the Palestinian problem plays a role of false witness. . . ."

"Precision in all things regarding the Zionist use of the Holocaust is vital. Important opinions on this matter are held by people who refuse to attach their name to the name of [French Holocaust denier Robert] Faurisson and his ilk. . . . Lebanon has too many fakes, and it does not need *The Protocols of the Elders of Beirut.*"

Also writing in *Al-Hayat* was columnist Abd Al-Wahhab Badrikhan, who focused not on Holocaust denial per se but on the damage the conference would do to Lebanon's image: "Some Arab intellectuals have condemned, and rightly so, the dubious call to convene a conference in Beirut with the aim of casting doubt upon the Jewish Holocaust [carried out] by the Nazis. . . . While this conference will make no impression on the issue of the Holocaust, the damage caused to Lebanon will be certain. Lebanon aspires today to tackle its economic crisis, and for this it needs international economic institutions. Thus, this clandestine conference, which may be no more than a political move or Internet maneuver, will thwart Lebanese efforts, even if it can be assumed that this is not one of the goals that fill the heads of the anonymous participants. . . ."

In early March 2001, the U.S. State Department asked the Lebanese government to cancel the conference. Initially, the Lebanese government denied all knowledge of the upcoming conference, but following increased American pressure, on March 23, Lebanese Prime Minister Rafiq Hariri announced its cancellation.

Saudi Editor Apologizes for Publishing Blood Libel

In March 2002, the Saudi government daily *Al-Riyadh* published a blood libel [in which allegations of ritual murder are made against a religion] authored by Dr. Umayma Ahmad Al-Jalahma of King Faysal University in Al-Dammam, Saudi Arabia, that included a graphic description of how Jews supposedly murdered non-Jewish youths to obtain blood for pastries for the Purim holiday. The article, which appeared in translation in the Western media, was harshly criticized in the U.S. Following condemnation by Congress, the U.S. State Department, and even President [George W.] Bush himself, the newspaper's editor, Turki Al-Sudeiri, a member of the Saudi royal family, published an apology for the article and fired its author. In his apology, Al-Sudeiri wrote: "I checked the article and found it not fit for publication because it was not based on scientific or historical facts, and it even contradicted the rituals of all the known religions in the world, including Hinduism and Buddhism.". . .

"In Israel itself there are moderate Jews such as Yisrael Shahak, who fought Zionist racism and exposed it in many of his studies. There are others like Shahak, and our dispute with phenomena such as [Israeli prime minister Ariel] Sharon must in no way cause us to generalize the emotions of hatred to all Jews. Furthermore, in principle, an idiotic and false news item regarding the use of human blood in the food of other human beings, whoever they may be, should not be published, since this does not exist in the world at all. . . ."

Criticism of Antisemitic Series on Egyptian Television

During the month of Ramadan (November–December) 2002, Egyptian and other television stations across the Arab world aired a 41-part Egyptian-produced television series called "Horseman Without a Horse" based on the notorious forgery *The Protocols of the Elders of Zion*. The broadcast of the series sparked an internal debate in the Arab media, due particularly to the publicity the series received in the West. Most of those contributing to the debate praised the series' producer for his "national" work of art. Yet as more episodes were screened, Western pressure increased. The pressure included a request from the U.S. State Department to the Egyptian government to stop the series from being aired. As the pressure rose, more and more Arab intellectuals condemned the series' use of the *Protocols* and stated that they were a forgery.

The Egyptian Organization for Human Rights condemned the broadcasts, saying that while freedom of expression and artistic freedom must be protected, these freedoms must not be exploited "to propagate events that might incite hatred based on religion, race, color, or gender." The organization stressed that most historians had made it clear that the *Protocols* were a fake, and demanded that the Arab television networks airing the series note this fact to the viewers, thus "respecting the Arab citizen's right to receive the correct information." Organization secretary-general Hafez Abu Sa'adeh told *The Associated Press:* "Supporting the Palestinian cause doesn't need forged *Protocols*. What is happening on the ground [in the Palestinian territories] is more reprehensible than anything else."

The secretary-general of the Palestinian Information Ministry, Ahmad Dahbour, wrote: ". . . The *Protocols of the Elders of Zion* are a stupid pamphlet full of nonsense, that depicts an international conference of the [forces of] evil, led by yellow-faced people capable of grasping the world in their hands . . . like a boiled egg and squashing it. The conflict with the Zionist enterprise is graver and more dangerous than these nonsensical words. If we do not present Zionism as it is—a nationalistic, racist European movement that emerged at the periphery of the old colonialism and imperialism—we will make ourselves easy prey. . . . "

Writing in *Al-Hayat's* movie column, Ibrahim Al-Arabi opposed the airing of the series: ". . . By means of the series, the art of Arab television managed to place itself at the heart of a lengthy debate, going back over 150 years, about the book, which today is known with certainty to be a 'fabrication' by the Russian Czar's secret police aimed at justifying attacks on the Russian Jews. This book always served fascist, racist, and antisemitic regimes, for stepping up persecution of the Jews—with a more disastrous result for the Arabs than for the Jews.

> *In December 2002, [Egyptian] President Mubarak's political advisor Osama Al-Baz . . . debunked some of the most notorious antisemitic myths, particularly the* Protocols, *the blood libel, and Holocaust denial.*

The Egyptian government officials' argument that they could not stop the program from being aired because Egypt guaranteed freedom of expression was also rejected by the Arab intellectuals.

Following pressure levied from different directions, Egyptian Television decided to replace the original opening sequence declaring, "Some of the events [depicted here] are real, and some are imaginary; some have already taken place, and some will take place in the future," with one that, while it did not completely rule out the possibility that the *Protocols* were authentic, clarified that the series "is not aimed at proving the authenticity of the so-called *Protocols of the Elders of Zion*, which have not been historically proven to be correct. . . ." Furthermore, the foreword in a new edition of *The Protocols of the El-*

ders of Zion, published in Egypt in July 2002 following great viewer interest in the series, refers to the possibility that the *Protocols* are a forgery. The foreword explains the view that the *Protocols* are a secret Jewish plan to take over the world, but also sets out "a different approach, found particularly in the West and among Jewish intellectuals," that "the *Protocols* are an example of racist literature and hate literature."

Mubarak's Advisor Refutes Racist Myths

American congressmen's harsh reactions to the series led to an Egyptian response on the highest diplomatic level. In December 2002, President Mubarak's political advisor Osama Al-Baz published a series of articles in the Egyptian government daily *Al-Ahram* in which he offered an extensive analysis of antisemitism, debunked some of the most notorious antisemitic myths, particularly the *Protocols*, the blood libel, and Holocaust denial, and stated that antisemitism originated in Europe and not in the Arab or Muslim world.

"With regard to the false *Protocols*," Al-Baz explains in his analysis, "there is a great deal of proof and evidence showing that these *Protocols* are forged." He sets out in detail historical research findings regarding their origin, and states: "Anyone who looks through these *Protocols* carefully will easily find two important facts: First, most of the topics to which the *Protocols* refer are completely Russian . . . which shows that the author of the false documents was Russian in his concepts and interest, and that he expressed the opinion of the Russian ruling class during the last years of its rule. Second, the *Protocols* make the Jews simultaneously responsible for something and for its opposite. They are responsible for good and evil, for revolution and counterrevolution, for capitalism and communism. . . ."

"In addition," he continues, "it should be taken into account that Hitler used these false *Protocols* to incite the German people against the Jews, and to claim that they are conspiring against it, destroying the German economy, and acting to bring down the foundations of the state by conspiring with foreign elements because they are disloyal to the state in which they live. All this [he did] so as to attain his goal, which was essentially to purge Germany and the countries it conquered of Jews. This caused the physical destruction of many of Europe's Jews."

"With regard to the story of the matza [mixed with] blood, which is used by many to this very day," Al-Baz states, "it began with accusing the Jews of customarily murdering a Christian, preferably a child, during Easter in order to mock the Messiah on the holiday marking His crucifixion. . . . This accusation spread every time a Christian child disappeared. It was enough for someone to say they saw the child near the Jewish neighborhood for some of the Jews in the neighborhood to be accused of murdering the boy, and taking his blood to be offered as a sacrifice or for [medical] treatment. The punishment for this charge was usually extremely cruel, and usually led to the hanging of the accused." Al-Baz added, "No one said that an incident of this kind took place in a Muslim country, except for the case that it is claimed happened in Damascus in 1840 . . . but no one can present sufficient evidence to prove it. . . ."

> *Our [Muslim] religion prohibits us from aggression and injustice, and teaches us to live in brotherhood with others as long as they desire the same.*

Al-Baz also specifically mentions some anti-Jewish slogans of Muslim origin, and says that their use is wrong. "It is not in the interests of the Palestinian cause and the Palestinian people that some among us repeat slogans that threaten Jews, such as '*Khybar, Khybar, Yah Yahud, jaysh Muhammad saya'ud* (Khybar, Oh Jews, Muhammad's army will return).' The army of Islam during the time of the Messenger [Muhammad], and during the time of the righteous Caliphs, [and the rulers] who came after them, did not threaten the Jews and did not frighten peaceful people; rather, it responded to aggression, prevented damage [to Islam], and defended the Muslim land and their rights. . . . Our religion prohibits us from aggression and injustice, and teaches us to live in brotherhood with others as long as they desire the same. . . ."

"Each one of us [Arabs] must know that when he harms the Jews collectively as a race or as a people—and thus presents himself as one who expresses inhuman racist approaches that are outmoded—he harms the interests of his nation."

In his articles, Al-Baz also differentiated between criticism of Israel and antisemitism, and states, "Anyone who criticizes Israel does not need antisemitic claims to reveal the damage necessarily caused by its policy. . . ."

In his recommendations to the Arab side on how to improve relations with Israel and the Jews, Al-Baz emphasized that "the mistake is to say that all the Jews are evil or good, and that by belonging to the Jewish religion they are implicitly guilty of certain faults or necessarily must behave differently than others." Similarly, Al-Baz explains that the Arabs must distinguish between Jews and Zionists, and realize that not every Jew is a Zionist or Israeli and that there is disagreement even among Israelis, and not all are extremists.

> **In March 2003, Al-Azhar University's Institute for Islamic Research issued a recommendation not to describe contemporary Jews as 'apes and pigs.'**

He called on the Arabs to stop interpreting matters relating to the Jews in terms of conspiracy, to stop expressing sympathy for Hitler and Nazism, and not to use the symbol of the Star of David in drawings and cartoons critical of Israeli policy and officials. This, he says, is because Israel is very sensitive about this symbol, "which arouses in the Jews painful memories [of the yellow patch of the Nazi era] and symbolizes the height of repression, terror, and racism."

Al-Baz also objects to the use of the common anti-Jewish slur "apes and pigs," saying, "We must not make improper use of the Koran by describing the Jews as the sons of apes and pigs, as it is clear that the words of the Koran on the matter of this metamorphosis do not mean that all the Children of Israel or the Jews were punished with this punishment. . . . Similarly, we do not know for certain whether the transformation was physical or used as a metaphor and an image. . . ."

Stop Calling Jews "Apes and Pigs"

In March 2003, Al-Azhar University's Institute for Islamic Research issued a recommendation not to describe contemporary Jews as "apes and pigs." The meeting during which the recommendation was drafted was headed by Sunni Islam's highest-ranking cleric, the sheikh of Al-Azhar, Muhammad Sayyed Tantawi.

Calling Jews "apes and pigs" is very common in the anti-semitic discourse of the Arab world, particularly in Islamist circles. For the most part, the term is used as a synonym for Jews, or in strings of epithets originating in the Koran and Muslim tradition regarding Jews. Sheikh Tantawi himself, in an April 2002 sermon, called Jews "the enemies of Allah, the sons of apes and pigs."

According to reports on *Al-Bawaba* and in *Al-Watan*, Al-Azhar's discussion on calling Jews "apes and pigs" followed a request to the Islamic Research Institute from the Egyptian Foreign Ministry to examine the matter. This request came after the Egyptian Embassy in Washington, D.C., reported that there was anger in American society over Muslim preachers and clerics calling Jews these names.

Also, as noted above, three months before, Osama Al-Baz criticized calling Jews "apes and pigs" in his series of articles in *Al-Ahram*.

[Since 2001], there has been a change in the attitude of some shapers of Arab public opinion towards antisemitic statements. This change may reflect the impact of translating material from the Arab media into Western languages. This exposure of the material in the Western media, and the resulting criticism in the West, particularly the U.S., in the media, government, and Congress, induces shapers of Arab public opinion to back down from their antisemitic stances—or at least to refrain from making antisemitic statements.

It also appears that the increase in antisemitic propaganda in the Arab media since the beginning of the *Al-Aqsa Intifada* [Palestinian uprising in 2000] has led some Arab intellectuals to rethink the matter and reject antisemitic statements. Some have expressed total objection to antisemitic ideas, explaining that they are based on false accusations of the Jews. Others reject antisemitic propaganda out of practical considerations, realizing that being perceived as antisemitic and, even more, as propagating antisemitism harms both the Arab image and Arab chances of gaining positive international public opinion.

It is still too early to say whether this is an ongoing and consistent trend among some Arab intellectuals or merely passing statements, and whether these critical stances will change the nature of the anti-Jewish discourse in the Arab world.

Organizations to Contact

The editors have compiled the following list of organizations concerned with the issues debated in this book. The descriptions are derived from materials provided by the organizations. All have publications or information available for interested readers. The list was compiled on the date of publication of the present volume; the information provided here may change. Be aware that many organizations take several weeks or longer to respond to inquiries, so allow as much time as possible.

American Council For Judaism (ACJ)
PO Box 9009, Alexandria, VA 22304
(703) 836-2546
Web site: www.acjna.org

The council is dedicated to the advancement of Judaism as a religion of universal values that is in accord with the ideals of a democratic society. Resources found on its Web site include numerous articles on anti-Semitism and Zionism and a moderated message board that promotes dialogue on issues of concern to the American Jewish community. ACJ publishes the bimonthly *Special Interest Report* (*SIR*) and *ISSUES*, a quarterly journal.

American-Israeli Cooperative Enterprise (AICE)
2810 Blaine Dr., Chevy Chase, MD 20815
(301) 565-3918 • fax: (301) 587-9056
e-mail: mgbard@aol.com • Web site: www.us-israel.org

AICE seeks to strengthen the U.S.-Israel relationship by emphasizing values the two nations have in common and developing cooperative social and educational programs that address shared domestic problems. It also works to enhance Israel's image by publicizing novel Israeli solutions to these problems. It publishes the book *Partners for Change: How U.S.-Israel Cooperation Can Benefit America*, and its Web site contains resources on responding to anti-Semitism.

Anti-Defamation League (ADL)
823 United Nations Plaza, New York, NY 10017
(212) 490-2525
Web site: www.adl.org

The Anti-Defamation League's mission is "to stop, by appeals to reason and conscience and . . . by appeals to law, the defamation of the Jewish people." ADL is an international human rights organization that works to fight anti-Semitism, racism, and prejudice through education, legislation, litigation, and communication. ADL legal experts have drafted model hate crime legislation that has served as the basis for hate crime laws in over forty states. It publishes an annual report on anti-Semitism throughout the world.

B'nai B'rith
2020 K St. NW, 7th Fl., Washington, DC 20006
(202) 857-6600
Web site: http://bnaibrith.org

One of the oldest Jewish human rights organizations, B'nai B'rith has funded the construction of hospitals, orphanages, libraries, and housing for seniors. It serves in over fifty nations to protect the rights of Jews and to raise awareness about anti-Semitism. Its publications include the magazine *Jewish Monthly* as well as reports on anti-Semitic terrorism.

Committee for Accuracy in Middle East Reporting in America (CAMERA)
PO Box 428, Boston, MA 02258
(617) 789-3672
Web site: www.camera.org

CAMERA is a nonprofit media-watch organization "devoted to promoting accurate and balanced coverage of Israel and the Middle East." Through its student-oriented magazine, *CAMERA on Campus*, it seeks to educate students about Israel and Middle East issues as well as assist students who encounter anti-Semitic publications, speech, or acts.

International Fellowship of Christians and Jews (IFCJ)
30 N. La Salle St., Suite 2600, Chicago, IL 60602-3356
(800) 486-8844
Web site: www.ifcj.org

Founded in 1983 to promote greater communication, understanding, and cooperation between Jews and Christians, the fellowship, based in Chicago and Jerusalem, also builds support for Israel. IFCJ writers author press releases and editorials on topics such as the religious persecution of Jews and Christians. The Center for Jewish and Christian Values, a program of IFCJ, works to improve tolerance and the moral climate of America through the common moral principles of Jews and Christians.

Jewish Defense League (JDL)
PO Box 480370, Los Angeles, CA 90048
(818) 980-8535
Web site: www.jdl.org

JDL is an activist organization that openly confronts anti-Semitism and neo-Nazi organizations. Its members believe that Jews should take an active stance in combating anti-Semitic speech and acts. The JDL Web site contains news on anti-Semitic groups, Internet hate propaganda, as well as information on Jewish culture.

Simon Wiesenthal Center
1399 South Roxbury, Los Angeles, CA 90035
(800) 900-9036
Web site: www.wiesenthal.com

The Simon Wiesenthal Center, founded in 1977, is an international Jewish rights organization that works to fight anti-Semitism and intolerance around the globe. It is also concerned with such issues as the

Holocaust, neo-Nazism, and hate on the Internet. It publishes an annual report, *Digital Terrorism and Hate*, which catalogues over four thousand Internet Web sites that spread anti-Semitic hate propaganda and terrorism. It also publishes the quarterly magazine *Response* and has a library of materials on the Holocaust, genocide, and racism that it makes available to students.

Vidal Sassoon International Center for the Study of Antisemitism (SICSA)
Hebrew University of Jerusalem
Mount Scopus Campus, Jerusalem, Israel
972-2-5882494
Web site: http://sicsa.huji.ac.il

The center is a research-oriented institution that undertakes to understand anti-Semitism, focusing on relations between Jews and non-Jews in situations of conflict and crisis. SICSA publishes an annual report in addition to papers on its research that appear in *Analysis of Current Trends in Antisemitism* and *Studies in Antisemitism*.

Bibliography

Books

Doris Bergen — *War & Genocide: A Concise History of the Holocaust.* Lanham, MD: Rowman & Littlefield, 2003.

William Brustein — *Roots of Hate: Anti-Semitism in Europe Before the Holocaust.* Cambridge, UK: Cambridge University Press, 2003.

Frederick B. Davis — *The Jew and Deicide: The Origin of an Archetype.* Lanham, MD: University Press of America, 2003.

Daniel Jonah Goldhagen — *A Moral Reckoning: The Role of the Catholic Church in the Holocaust and Its Unfulfilled Duty of Repair.* New York: Alfred A. Knopf, 2002.

Steven L. Jacobs — *Dismantling the Big Lie: The Protocols of the Elders of Zion.* Los Angeles: Simon Wiesenthal Center, 2003.

Peter Laufer — *Exodus to Berlin: The Return of the Jews to Germany.* Chicago: Ivan R. Dee, 2003.

Jerome S. Legge — *Jews, Turks, and Other Strangers: The Roots of Prejudice in Modern Germany.* Madison: University of Wisconsin Press, 2003.

Leon Poliakov — *The History of Anti-Semitism.* Philadelphia: University of Philadelphia Press, 2003.

Jose M. Sanchez — *Pius XII and the Holocaust: Understanding the Controversy.* Washington, DC: Catholic University of America Press, 2002.

Gabriel Schoenfield — *The Return of Anti-Semitism.* San Francisco: Encounter, 2004.

John Weiss — *The Politics of Hate: Anti-Semitism, History, and the Holocaust in Modern Europe.* Chicago: Ivan R. Dee, 2003.

Periodicals

Tewfik Allal — "A Muslim Manifesto from France," *Dissent*, Summer 2004.

Barbara Amiel — "A Plague Without a Cure," *Maclean's*, March 8, 2004.

Brian Bethune — "New Old Hatred," *Maclean's*, August 2, 2004.

Christianity Today — "The Longest Hatred," April 2004.

Jean Bethke Elshtain   "Anti-Semitism or Anti-Judaism?" *Christian Century*, May 5, 2004.

Karen Evans   "The Middle Eastern World," *College & Research Libraries News*, October 2004.

Jonathan Gatehouse   "Pride and Prejudice," *Maclean's*, August 2, 2004.

David Gespass   "On Being Jewish," *Guild Notes*, Spring 2004.

Irving Greenberg   "Anti-Semitism in 'The Passion,'" *Commonweal*, May 7, 2004.

Jamey Keaton   "Web War and Anti-Semites," *Times Educational Supplement*, April 2, 2004.

Neil J. Kressel   "The Urgent Need to Study Islamic Anti-Semitism," *Chronicle of Higher Education*, March 12, 2004.

Shalom Lappin   "The Need for a New Jewish Politics," *Dissent*, Summer 2004.

Michael Lerner   "Criticism of AIPAC Is Not Anti-Semitism," *America*, October 4, 2004.

Simon Montefiore   "A Dangerous Time to Be a Jew," *New Statesman*, June 28, 2004.

Rabbi Marc Schneier   "Dr. King's Legacy and Anti-Semitism," *New York Amsterdam News*, January 22, 2004.

Donald Senior   "Blame the Gospels?" *Commonweal*, May 7, 2004.

Andrew Solomon   "The Loneliness of a Liberal US Jew," *New Statesman*, October 25, 2004.

UN Chronicle   "Anti-Semitism Has Been a Harbinger of Discrimination Against Others," June/August 2004.

UN Chronicle   "Confronting Anti-Semitism," June/August 2004.

Kevin Whitelaw   "Fighting the Flames of Hate," *U.S. News & World Report*, May 10, 2004.

Elie Wiesel   "Pope John Paul II: Pointing the Way to Reconciliation," *Time*, April 26, 2004.

Cathy Young   "Hating Jews," *Reason*, February 2004.

Carlyn Zwarenstein   "Drawing the Line on Anti-Semitism," *Canadian Dimension*, May/June 2004.

Index

109